"But I thou
was your ...

"I mean, that's wha........... ....., ...an went on, to cover her embarrassment. "When Zelda said Jake and Carrie McCabe were coming to dinner, it sounded like that. I would never have guessed you had a twelve-year-old daughter. She's a lovely girl...." Her voice trailed off; instead of lessening her discomfort, she seemed to have made it worse.

He was watching her across the table in an odd, intense way. "I had a wife once," he said, his tone cold and distant. "We met in college. Married young. Unfortunately, as it turned out, she didn't like country life—or, it appears, country vets. She's a career woman now. A real city person. Her whole life revolves around her job. Rather like you, I imagine."

"I didn't mean to pry," Hannah said quickly, though she was angry at his casual assumption. "But really, you haven't the faintest idea what I'm like."

His mouth tucked in at one corner. "I'd be surprised if I'm wrong."

Hannah flushed and looked away, wondering why it mattered what this man thought of her, why she wanted to prove him wrong. Because, strangely enough, she did....

Amanda Clark is the pseudonym for the mother-daughter writing team of Janet O'Daniel and Amy Midgley. They began collaborating on romances long-distance, when they lived in different states. Now they've both moved to South Carolina, which makes working together a lot less complicated. Besides writing, Amy manages the office of a large animal clinic, and she's co-written a handbook for veterinary office staff, a background that accounts for the authentic descriptions of the hero's work in *City Girl, Country Girl*. And both Amy and Janet have been newspaper reporters, which no doubt explains why the story's heroine is a journalist!

CITY GIRL, COUNTRY GIRL

Amanda Clark

Harlequin Books

TORONTO • NEW YORK • LONDON
AMSTERDAM • PARIS • SYDNEY • HAMBURG
STOCKHOLM • ATHENS • TOKYO • MILAN

ISBN 0-373-03104-1

Harlequin Romance first edition February 1991

CITY GIRL, COUNTRY GIRL

CHAPTER ONE

HANNAH PUT HER FOOT on the brake as she drove the sleek low Porsche into the little village. Harrison Falls, the tiny letters on the map said. She looked around curiously. Huge old maples and oaks sheltered houses set far back from the road. Most were painted white and had dark green shutters. Slate sidewalks meandered in front of them. She glanced at a sign that read Bridge Street, and now Hannah could see it—a bridge with black iron railings spanning a creek that ran through the center of town, probably on its way to the big lake she'd seen on the outskirts.

The town had an undeniable beauty. Her editor, Bob Anderson, had been right about that, anyway. "You're due for a vacation," he'd urged that day as she sat in his office. "And this sounds like a great place. It's upstate in the lake country. Nice and quiet. Ed Franklin in advertising told me about it. He rents a place there every summer."

She remembered her impatience, remembered how she had tossed her dark hair back over her shoulder and rhythmically swung one foot in its high-heeled shoe. "Nice and quiet? What do I need with nice and quiet? Are you trying to get rid of me, Bob?"

"Just trying to get you to take some time off. They won't be calling you to testify for at least six weeks."

Hannah pulled the car over to the curb now and consulted the note he had scrawled on the margin of her map. "Bridge St 2 blks. Turn left on Bender's Rd." She started the car again and drove slowly, looking for road signs.

"You're worried about me, I can tell," she had told him accusingly that day. "You think I'm too visible."

"Not at all!" Anderson had protested, a bit too loudly. "Only I have to admit, it isn't every reporter who uncovers corruption in the construction business and involves everyone from crooked building inspectors to millionaire contractors. *And* gets herself in the running for a Pulitzer." He grinned at her as she sat there with her long legs crossed, her gray eyes studying him critically. "Or if they do, they don't generally look as good as you."

Hannah ignored this. "I'm not afraid, you know," she had insisted.

"Didn't say you were. But wouldn't this be a great chance to work on that in-depth series you've been wanting to do on grass-roots political activity? Perfect spot for it." He flung both hands out in a gesture of exasperation. "Look, be a good kid and do what I say. Just this once," he added meaningfully.

Hannah had sighed deeply. "Oh, all right. But only because you're dangling that carrot in front of my nose about the new series. Where is this place, anyway?"

Bender's Road—there it was. Hannah turned left, still driving slowly, examining houses and names on mailboxes.

"Here, I'll show you," Bob Anderson had said, quickly producing a map. "I've even found a place for you to stay. House owned by a lady named Zelda Miles."

Hannah's smooth eyebrows had shot up in a question. "Isn't there some kind of apartment...maybe a condo I could sublet..."

"This is a big old place, I understand. You'll have plenty of room and lots of privacy."

"You're sure?" Hannah had asked doubtfully.

"Trust me, Hannah. Just trust me," he'd said with a groan.

Now, on the right, Hannah saw a large house—white with green shutters like the others—on the very edge of town, just where the slate sidewalk ended. It had a porch with wicker chairs and a hammock, and the mailbox in front said Z. Miles. Hannah turned carefully into a dirt lane with grass growing in its center. She parked and got out, climbed the three steps to the porch and rang the doorbell. She could hear the bell ringing inside, but no one came to the door. She pressed the bell again. Still no one. Hannah's eyebrows came together in a frown. Bob Anderson had said it was all arranged. She was expected. Suddenly the fresh spring day became warm and oppressive. She was desperate for a long soaking bath, a change of clothes. She gave the bell another impatient jab. Then she turned and began looking around. The nearest house was at least a hundred yards away. She could just glimpse it through the trees. And there seemed to be someone moving around. Crossly, she strode down the steps and struck off across the lawn.

No fence divided the two properties, but there was a line of shrubs and trees that Hannah managed to wriggle through, scratching her suede skirt and pulling her silk blouse awry. Angrily, she paused to tuck her blouse back in, then glanced about, hoping to spot some sign of life. Whoever had been there had now disappeared. The big yard was behind a large old house, and there was a pile of boxes, set off the ground and stacked in an orderly fashion, rather like chests of drawers. While she hesitated, a man appeared, followed by a golden retriever. The man went to one of the boxes, lifted the top and began sprinkling something that looked like powdered sugar into the box. He was tall and muscular, wearing jeans and a plaid workshirt, the sleeves rolled up past his elbows. His sandy hair fell forward as he bent in concentration over what he was doing.

"Excuse me," Hannah said in a loud clear voice.

At once the dog went into action, and lunged toward her. One of the piles of boxes wobbled perilously as he knocked against it, and in the next instant two large muddy paws had been planted squarely on the pale peach silk of her blouse. Hannah let out a cry of alarm and toppled over backward into soft moist dirt. There was an angry buzzing sound and something stung her on the cheekbone. Hannah screamed. Distantly she could hear a man's voice swearing. Then there was a moment of total confusion as the pain of the sting mingled with the soft moist caress of a large tongue licking her, while in the background she had a dim sense of the tilting boxes being placed upright again. The man, now with a netted helmet on his head, ran to her and yanked her to her feet.

"Get away, Zack," he muttered angrily. "Damn! Who are you anyway? Here, let's get into the house."

"I'm hurt!" Hannah yelled. "What are those things? Bees? Why don't you have a sign warning people?"

"All right, come on, come on, this way." He was half dragging her up the steps and through the back door of the house. Hannah had a dim sense of being in a kitchen, roomy and old-fashioned, with a big round table in the middle covered by a red-and-white checked cloth. Then she was aware of one eye gradually closing as the bee sting swelled.

"Here. Sit down and I'll take care of that," the man said, pulling off the veiled hat and flinging it aside; then he strode to the sink to wash his hands. "Lord knows when I'll get to do the rest of that Terramycin," he grumbled. "And I promised Carrie I'd look after it today. I have people waiting in there already, and those bees are going to be so mad now I'll have to smoke them to quiet them down."

Hannah stared at him through one eye, trying to figure out what he was talking about, but he might as well have been speaking a foreign language. She could see now that he had a lean intense face, deep blue eyes and a firm jaw, and that he moved with no wasted motion—strongly and efficiently.

"I didn't know what they were," she said indignantly. "And even if I'd known... Does every little noise upset them that much?"

He returned to her and bent over her upturned face, pinching the stinger out neatly and then applying an ice cube wrapped in a dish towel. "There. Hold that in place," he ordered. "It isn't the noise that upsets them," he said. "Bees can't hear. It was Zack—the dog— whacking against the hives. It gave them a jolt and upset them. Generally he doesn't do things like that, but he was startled at seeing you." The chill of the ice cube was taking away some of the pain, but the swelling was still there. Hannah felt torn between fury and embarrassment. The man was gazing down at her, his face less angry now, more amused. She could see a dancing light in the blue eyes.

"I'm Jake McCabe," he said. "And you're from out of town, obviously."

"Hannah Chase. Yes. I'm from New York."

"Well, fine, Hannah Chase. Are you looking for someone?"

Hannah realized suddenly that her silk blouse had large paw prints on it, that her suede skirt was muddied and scratched, and that her pale suede pumps were black with the soft dirt where she had fallen. She drew herself up with what dignity she could muster, pushing back hair that had straggled down both sides of her face.

"I'm looking for a Mrs. Zelda Miles, who I believe is your neighbor."

"Oh—you're the one who's come to stay at Zelda's. I get it. Only she's not home."

"That I know," Hannah said witheringly. "I was wondering if you could tell me when she'll be back."

"Oh, Lord, I don't know. She and Carrie have gone out to some of the other hives. It might be a while."

Misery overcame dignity. "But I want a bath!" Hannah wailed. "I want to unpack! This is just so . . . so awful!"

He was staring at her with his forehead puckered as if he was trying to figure her out. "But why didn't you just go in? Zelda never locks her door. I'm sure she expected you to."

"She . . . expected me to?"

"Sure. And she probably left you a note. Zelda's always leaving notes around."

"Would it be all right? You're sure?"

"I'm sure. But now I'd better get going. I have a waiting room full of patients, and I've still got to get back to those bees later when they've quieted down some."

"You're a doctor?"

"A veterinarian."

"Oh. Well, thank you. I guess," Hannah added rather sourly, thinking privately that if it hadn't been for him none of this would have happened.

"Wait a minute. Let me take one more look at that." He leaned over her and gently touched the area around the sting. His face was so close to hers that Hannah could see the blue eyes quite clearly. A muscle in his jaw moved as if he was considering her in an analytical way—the way he might look at one of his patients, she thought.

"Keep the ice on it for a while. That'll help the swelling go down. You don't seem to have any allergic reaction to bees. Very few people do, actually. And after you've been stung a few more times, you'll hardly notice it."

"Thank you," Hannah said coldly. "I hadn't planned on any more close association with bees."

"You never know," he said breezily. He gave her a glance that took in the soiled blouse and smudged skirt. "If you need to have that stuff cleaned, I'll pay for it."

"Thank you. That won't be necessary." Hannah struggled to her feet. The man probably thought a five-dollar bill would cover the damage. Obviously he had no idea what it cost to have suede cleaned—if there was even a cleaner in Harrison Falls who could manage it, which she certainly doubted.

"Well, go ahead, make yourself at home over there," he said. "I've got to see my patients." He started out of the kitchen with the dog at his heels. When he reached the door he turned back. "Or you can wait here if you'd rather. Make yourself a cup of tea—or whatever."

"Thank you," she said again. "I believe I'll be going."

"Suit yourself."

"Will those bees attack me again?"

"Not likely."

His nonchalance was infuriating. Hannah got up and left the house, giving the hives a wide berth and squeezing through the shrubs once more, making decisions as she went. What she would do, she decided, was find other accommodations in town. It might take a day or more, so she would stay at this Zelda Miles's place until she found a hotel or apartment of some sort and then she would move herself into it. The whole atmosphere around her was altogether too casual and offhand for her taste. Not that she'd expected any red-carpet treatment, but to be left to shift for herself, get attacked by huge dogs and swarmed by bees hardly augured well for a peaceful holiday. The proximity of this veterinarian— had he told her his name? McCabe, that was it—was entirely too unpleasant. A bath and a night's rest and she'd start looking for a new place.

She arrived at Zelda Miles's house, climbed the porch steps again and this time she cautiously turned the doorknob. The big front door swung open and Hannah stepped inside.

She had an immediate impression of high ceilings, old-fashioned rooms, ferns in corners. The fragrance of recent baking hung in the air. And as the man had predicted, there was a note, taped to the newel post of the stairway in the big center hall. "Miss Chase. Make yourself at home. Your room is at the top of the stairs to the right. Bath adjoining. Back soon. Z. Miles."

Hannah stood staring at the note for a moment, then slowly shook her head as she tried to make sense of this unfamiliar way of doing business. But at last she returned to the car for her luggage and her lap-top computer and wearily mounted the stairs.

The room to which she'd been directed was enormous. It had a slightly worn flowered carpet and a high double bed—an antique, Hannah suspected—built of dark glossy wood. In addition to that, the place was furnished with heavy mahogany chairs, bureaus and tables, yet it seemed not at all crowded. A huge bay window overlooked the back lawn. Hannah pushed open the door to the "bath adjoining," where she saw a big white claw-footed tub, a pedestal sink, and on the floor a rag rug that looked homemade.

A bath, Hannah decided, might help matters.

There was plenty of hot water, and she soaked luxuriously, then slipped into a robe and lay down on the bed, which was surprisingly comfortable. She covered herself with a quilt she'd found folded up at the foot of the bed; it seemed to be handmade in some elaborate pattern. Hannah, who had once done a series on American folk arts, tried to identify it, but found herself growing sleepy instead. For a few moments she hung on to her thoughts—that man had really been maddening—but then felt herself slipping off. Like Goldilocks, she thought, in the three bears' house, and fell into blissful oblivion.

Someone was sitting beside the bed watching her when she woke up. A woman of fifty or so, thin and wiry, with a mop of unruly gray hair and a thrown-together look. Blue jeans, sweatshirt and a red-and-white striped apron covering both.

"Oh, good, you're awake," the woman said pleasantly. "I hope I didn't disturb you, but I'm glad you're not still sleeping, because I brought some tea for us. I looked in on you a few minutes ago, and you were dead to the world. That must have been a tiring drive up from the city."

Hannah struggled to a sitting position. Now she could
see that the light in the room had changed; shadows were
longer and there was a golden cast over everything.
"How do you do," she said, trying for dignity. "You
must be Mrs. Miles—"

"Zelda," the woman interrupted firmly. "And I know
your name's Hannah."

"Yes. How do you do. I hope it was all right, my
coming in like this."

Zelda brushed Hannah's concern away with a shake
of her head. "Here. Have some tea." She handed her a
delicate china cup and slightly mismatched saucer. The
tea was dark and fragrant, with a tiny sliver of lemon.
Hannah sipped it slowly. She should probably mention
to the woman that she'd be staying only temporarily....

"Sorry I was out when you got here," Zelda Miles
said. She gave Hannah a closer look. "Oh, goodness,
what happened? Did you get stung? Little swelling there
under one eye. Well, no matter, it'll go down soon. What
it was, you see, I had to help Carrie with some of her
hives. Spring's a busy time with the bees, and she counts
on me. I'm glad you made yourself at home."

"Carrie?"

"Yes, Carrie McCabe, from next door."

"Oh, I see. I met Mr.—Dr. McCabe."

"Did you! Oh, yes, that's probably how you got
stung." Zelda seemed to regard this as of no impor-
tance. "Well, you're just real welcome here, that's what
I wanted to tell you. You're a newspaper writer, aren't
you? That's what I understood."

"Yes. And I'll be doing some writing while I'm here.
I'll try to keep out of your way, though." Now why had
she said that? No need, really, to do any explaining,
since she wouldn't be staying long.

"Oh, that's lovely. And real exciting," Zelda said. "You just make believe it's your own house."

Hannah fingered the edge of the quilt. "This is lovely," she said. "Is it a family heirloom?"

Zelda Miles hooted. "That old thing? Lordy, no! Just made that one winter when we had a lot of snow and I didn't get out much. It's the 'bear paw' pattern. Well, I'd better get started on supper. Come down whenever you're ready."

"Oh, I wouldn't dream of— That is, I wasn't planning to eat here. That would be much too much work for you," Hannah stammered.

"Why? I've got to eat, too, you know. Besides, I like company. We're having some tonight. No trouble to set two or three extra places."

"Guests? Tonight?" Hannah echoed in dismay.

"Just Jake and Carrie McCabe. Come down whenever you feel like it."

She collected the cups and was gone before Hannah could protest again. Hannah got up hurriedly and smoothed the bed, then stood in the middle of the room debating with herself. She felt she was here under false colors, since she didn't intend to stay. But of course she would pay for whatever time she did remain here; that went without saying. And the bed *was* comfortable. Plenty of hot bath water, and the dark tea with the faint tang of lemon had been delicious. Perhaps she would stick it out just long enough to rest up and get her bearings, get acquainted with the town a little. No need to rush, after all.

But if this was to be a dinner with company, what should she wear? People in Harrison Falls probably didn't dress up much. Something casual would be right, then. She unpacked a jumpsuit of soft turquoise silk—

one of her favorites. She'd bought it in Paris last year when she'd done a story on the French fashion industry.

She sat down at the big old-fashioned dressing table and began brushing her hair, leaning close to the mirror to see how much the swelling of the bee sting had gone down. And as she brushed, an odd unexpected thought kept nudging its way into her mind. Why did it bother her just the tiniest bit that Jake McCabe was coming to dinner—with his wife?

SHE NEED NOT HAVE WORRIED about the matter of dress, she realized when she got downstairs, for Zelda Miles obviously intended to remain just as she was for the occasion.

"Oh, say, don't you look the prettiest," Zelda said as she came bustling out of the kitchen, still in jeans, sweatshirt and apron. "Now sit right down and be comfortable while I finish up in here. Jake and Carrie'll be over soon."

"Couldn't I give you a hand with something?" Hannah asked.

Zelda looked, not unkindly, at the turquoise silk, the thin-strap sandals, the gold chain with its small winking diamond, and said, "I don't think so, dear. Everything's just about ready, anyway. I'm going to put biscuits in the oven and that'll be it."

Hannah glanced at the television set in one corner. "May I turn that on and see if I can get the evening news?"

Zelda laughed good-naturedly. "Well, you could try, but I'm afraid nothing much would happen. It broke last winter sometime and I never did see about getting it fixed. I've been meaning to, but something always seems to get in the way.''

"Oh, it's quite all right," Hannah said hastily.

"There—I think I hear Jake and Carrie, anyway," Zelda said, tilting her head to listen. "They always come in the back door. Yoo-hoo! We're in here," she called out.

Hannah turned toward the door that appeared to lead from the lofty old living room to the back of the house and saw it pushed open for two people to enter—Jake McCabe, now in a clean white shirt and fresh jeans, and a young girl of twelve or so, sandy-haired and freckled, with a small uptilted nose and wide blue eyes of a shade that matched McCabe's. She, too, was in jeans, and her yellow T-shirt bore a large picture of a bee.

"Well! Good evening. All settled in, I see," Jake McCabe said. The young girl was staring in wide-eyed wonder at Hannah's turquoise jumpsuit.

"You've met Jake, haven't you?" Zelda said, quickly taking over. "And this is his daughter, Carrie. Honey, this is Miss Hannah Chase from New York City. She's a writer, and she's going to be staying in Harrison Falls for a few weeks."

Carrie McCabe stepped forward and extended her hand. "How do you do," she said politely.

Hannah smiled at her. "Do I understand you're the one in charge of the bees?"

"Yes. I'm sorry you got stung. Dad told me about it."

"I seem to be recovering very well. I don't think very many young girls have bees as a hobby, though."

"Oh, they're not a hobby," Carrie said earnestly. "They're a business venture."

She said it seriously, and Hannah kept her own reply equally serious. "Is that so? How many hives do you have?"

"Not very many. Only thirty. Some in back of our house and the rest on farms around here. I give the farmers some honey after the harvest—for payment. But they like to have my bees on their land because it improves their crops. They say that's their real payment."

"Well now, sit down all of you, while I finish things up in the kitchen," Zelda said.

"I'll help, Zelda," Carrie offered at once, and the two of them disappeared through the door.

Jake McCabe dropped into a worn-looking armchair. "You happen to have arrived at a very busy time in the bee business," he said, and Hannah noticed how small crinkles appeared at the corners of his eyes when he smiled.

"Is that so?"

"Yes, cleaning out after winter, inspecting the hives, medicating, and now we're about to start re-queening. Some of the hives need a new queen in the spring. That's why I was pressed into service with the Terramycin today. There isn't enough time for Carrie to get to all her hives after school and on weekends, so the rest of us have to pitch in."

"Medicating?" Hannah's eyebrows lifted.

"Yes. For foulbrood. A disease that can wipe out a whole colony of bees. Terramycin acts as a preventive."

Hannah was once more experiencing the feeling of being an alien in a strange land, where the inhabitants took for granted matters of which she was entirely ignorant. Yet her reporter's instinct was at work.

"It sounds like a good story," she said. "With pictures of Carrie and all that stuff about bees. I'm sure some magazine would be interested."

"Oh, well," he said casually. "We don't care much about things like that."

Things like what? Hannah wondered. Publicity? The outside world? Or was it just a subtle putdown of her own life and what she did for a living?

She gave a little shrug. "I'm afraid I've been guilty of considering bees as just . . . bugs."

"Oh, sure, they are. But they're also complex characters in a complex society. Very interesting when you get to know them."

Hannah nodded. "I'll take your word for that," she said wryly. "My first close encounter wasn't a huge success." She found her mind working curiously around the matter of the McCabe household. A twelve-year-old daughter, but no wife? Obviously there had once been one. Was McCabe a widower, or was he divorced?

"There now," Zelda said, pushing the door open again. As a nod toward proper dinner attire she had discarded her red-and-white striped apron. "Biscuits in the oven, and you know how quick they are, so we might just as well sit down. Come along, everybody."

They ate in a dining room that was high-ceilinged and ferned like the living room. Pictures of fruit in bowls and ducks in flight hung in heavy frames on the walls, yet curiously, the effect was not oppressive but genial and homey. Zelda banged back and forth through a swinging door into the kitchen, fetching iced tea, homemade jam, extra butter. The menu would have made Hannah hesitate fastidiously back in New York—chicken with biscuits, gravy, stewed tomatoes. Here she found herself eating heartily, with an appetite that surprised her.

"Generally we eat in the kitchen, Hannah," Zelda explained. "This putting on the dog is all in honor of your arrival. After tonight it'll be back to normal."

"Tell us about what you do, Miss Chase," Carrie McCabe said, gazing at her and once again admiring the Paris jumpsuit.

"Oh, I write for a newspaper in New York. Mostly special-assignment articles where I have to do some investigative reporting. I've just finished a big project, so I'm taking a few weeks off. Only I brought my computer and I'm going to be working on other articles while I'm here."

Zelda shook her head in wonderment. "Hard for some people to close up shop when the day's over, isn't it? You probably just love your work and can't bear to leave it behind."

"Well—I am very used to being busy."

She was intensely aware of Jake McCabe's presence across the table, of his slow smile and the casual scrutiny he seemed to be giving her.

"Some people need their work to live. You know that, Zelda."

"Oh, I don't think that's how I'd describe myself," Hannah said, annoyed at his offhand assessment of her. "I have many other interests. I like concerts and the theater, reading—well, any number of things. But of course my work *is* important to me. Isn't yours to you?"

"Oh, sure. Except in a place like Harrison Falls, where the world is all around you, you can't help being involved in things besides work. The seasons mean more, for one thing. What's the difference between winter and spring in a big city, for instance?"

"The difference?" Hannah echoed blankly, feeling that she was being baited but not sure how to respond.

"Well, goodness—baseball, for one thing. And outdoor concerts, and— What do you mean, the difference?" she demanded crossly.

"Well, all I know is, around here spring means we have to get hopping," Zelda said matter-of-factly. "Carrie and I were really working this afternoon, weren't we? Found everything in fairly good shape, though. One hive not too prosperous, and a mouse had got into it, but a new queen'll fix that up. How soon do you think that mail-order batch will get here, Carrie?"

"You order bees by *mail?*" Hannah asked.

Carrie grinned. "Yes. Mr. Gretch, the postmaster, isn't too happy when they arrive. He usually calls and asks us to pick them up ourselves."

Zelda pushed herself up from the table. "Let's go fetch dessert and coffee, Carrie."

The two of them cleared away the plates and disappeared into the kitchen, where they could be heard chatting and moving around.

"Your daughter's a lovely girl," Hannah said. That much was true, even though she'd decided that McCabe himself had an annoyingly superior manner. She reached out to replace the top of the glass jam jar at the same instant he did, and their hands touched lightly. Hannah immediately pulled back and let him finish the job, surprised at the sudden shock the contact produced in her. "I thought at first," she went on quickly to cover her confusion, "that Carrie was your wife. Well, when Zelda said that Jake and Carrie were coming to dinner, it sounded like that. You know." Instead of lessening her discomfort, she seemed to have made it worse. He was watching her across the table in that odd intense way.

"I had a wife once," he said, his tone cold and distant. "We met in college. Married young. Unfortu-

nately, as it turned out, she didn't like the country life—
or country vets, it appeared. She's a career woman
now—like you, I imagine."

"I didn't mean to pry," Hannah said quickly, though
she was angry at his casual assumption. "But really, you
don't have the faintest idea what I'm like."

His mouth tucked in at one corner. "I'd be surprised
if I'm wrong," he said quietly.

Zelda and Carrie were back with dessert, for which
Zelda felt compelled to apologize.

"I had the biscuits, you see," she said. "And the
strawberries—well, they're not fresh, of course. Last
year's, but I had them in the freezer, so I just thought
we'd slap together some shortcake...."

The plates held towering creations of jewel-red berries, golden biscuits, whipped cream. In an expensive
New York restaurant, Hannah would have passed them
up after a horrified assessment of their calories. But just
this once, to be polite, she told herself. Again, she had
the impression that the man across the table was regard-
ing her with amusement.

Carrie gave her another admiring look and said dif-
fidently, "Miss Chase, your outfit's so pretty. Did it
come from a New York shop?"

Jake McCabe frowned. "That's very personal, Carrie."

"No, it's quite all right," Hannah interjected. "Only
I'd feel much more comfortable if you called me Hannah, Carrie. Actually I didn't buy it in New York. I
bought it in Paris when I was there on a story assign-
ment last year."

"Paris!" Carrie's eyes widened. "My mother sent me
something from Paris once. A dress."

"How wonderful," Hannah said, and in spite of herself glanced across the table at McCabe. His cocked eyebrows and small tight smile seemed to say, *See? I'm right about you.* Flushing, Hannah turned her attention back to her plate.

They had finished the shortcake and Carrie had poured coffee for them when the telephone rang. Zelda got up to answer it in the kitchen and almost at once poked her head back into the dining room. "For you, Jake. Frank Goodwin."

Hannah could hear his response through the door Zelda had left open. "What's up, Frank? Is it time? . . . Okay then. Bring her right in. I'll meet you there."

Still standing, Zelda took a quick swallow of coffee, then put down her cup as Jake returned. "Frank's corgi?" she asked.

He nodded. "Sorry, Zelda. I'm going to have to eat and run."

Carrie was on her feet, starting to clear dishes away hurriedly, but Zelda stopped her. "Never mind that, honey. Just leave everything. I'll take care of it later. Hannah, you'd better come with us. We're going to need all the hands we can muster. Unless I miss my guess, Frank Goodwin's going to collapse in the waiting room, and we may each have to take a puppy."

"Take a puppy . . . ?" Hannah repeated weakly.

"Yes. Jake's going to do a C-section on a corgi. Come on, come on, we're wasting time."

CHAPTER TWO

THEY TROOPED across to the McCabes' place next door, and now Hannah saw that there was a well-worn path between the houses and an opening in the hedge that was easy to pass through. This time they entered not through the kitchen but through a door at the side, which led into what looked like a well-equipped examining room and adjoining surgery.

"Keep an eye out for Frank, Zelda," Jake ordered. "He doesn't live that far away and he'll probably burn up the road to get here." Zelda nodded and disappeared through a door into what seemed to be a waiting room. Carrie had put on a white surgical coat and now passed one to Hannah.

"I don't know that I'll be very much help," Hannah stammered. "I'm not—that is, you know, not experienced in these things."

"I'll tell you what to do," Carrie reassured her. "You have to take care of each puppy individually, see, and sometimes they need attention. That's why it's good to have extra people on hand. Don't worry, I'll show you."

Jake was moving around easily, preparing instruments, assembling towels and a heating pad. Within minutes they heard the sound of screeching brakes outside, and then a stocky partially bald man who reminded Hannah of Bob Anderson came hurrying in with a blanket-wrapped bundle.

"You told me what to watch for, Jake," he said worriedly. "Is she going to be all right?"

"She's going to be fine, Frank," Jake said with a grin.

Zelda took the bundle from him and at once placed the dog on the operating table. Hannah saw the appeal in the large liquid eyes as the animal looked apprehensively at Jake.

"All right, Mitzi, steady now," he said, and put a comforting hand on her head. "Carrie? Ready to go with the anesthetic? Zelda, maybe you can get Frank settled in the kitchen with some coffee. We're going to need a box, too. I forgot that. Just dash out to the storage shed for one, will you, honey, while I get her ready?"

"Oh, please," Hannah interrupted. "Let Carrie go on with what she's doing. I'm sure I can find a box if you tell me where." The atmosphere of efficiency and even more, suspense, was making her jittery. She longed to be away from this room where everyone except her knew what to do.

He glanced at her, his eyes moving sardonically over the turquoise silk, the high-heeled sandals. "Okay, sure. It's right out at the back. Bikes and tools and stuff. We save boxes for things like this. They're on the shelf to your left as you go in."

Yanking on the white coat Carrie had given her, Hannah hurried out. She found the shed and in the twilight dimness she could see the things he had described, plus gasoline cans, a pump for bicycle tires, a lawn mower, a window fan covered with plastic. She glanced to the left and saw the shelf with boxes piled on it. She reached up and brought one down, then decided it looked inadequate. How many puppies would there be? She reached for another larger one and heard the ominous small sound of silk tearing as she caught the loose leg of the jumpsuit on something. A nail? She looked down apprehensively. Just below the white coat, she saw a jagged three-cornered tear right next to a large smudge of grease. She must have leaned against the bicycle that stood there near the wall. Hannah closed her eyes tightly as a flood of exasperation and utter despair swept over her. An $800 outfit, and this was the second one damaged. What was she doing scrambling around a toolshed in a place called Harrison Falls? Angrily, she seized the box and went hurrying back to the surgery.

Zelda had already returned from the kitchen, standing close to the table along with Jake McCabe and Carrie. Hannah shrank into the shadows and prayed no one would notice her. But Carrie was quick to glance her way.

"Oh, that's fine. Put it over there on the floor, will you, Hannah? Heating pad in it, covered with one of those towels. You can plug the heating pad in right there. Set it on medium and then lower it if it gets too warm."

Hannah hurried to obey, arranging heating pad and towel neatly. She plugged in the heating pad. How warm was medium? What was too warm? Fussing and testing, she was conscious all the time of the others in the room, their quiet presence, their teamwork efficiency.

"That looks good," Jake was saying. "Check her eyes now, Carrie."

"All the way under," Carrie said.

"Well, that's okay for now. We'll let her start to come out of it as soon as possible, though."

Zelda said, "Frank's pacing the floor in the kitchen. Talk about nervous fathers."

"Okay, here we go." There was silence for a few minutes, and Hannah drew back, keeping out of the way.

Then Jake's voice said, "Well, there, that looks good. Carrie, take the first one. Got a towel ready?"

"Ready."

Hannah watched in awe as Jake handed the girl something she at once wrapped in a towel, rubbing and cleaning it briskly.

"One for you, Zelda," said Jake. Zelda held a towel out and took the next one. "Yours breathing well, Carrie?"

"Just fine. Let me put him down." She carried the puppy to the heated box and returned. Hannah stared unbelievingly as it squirmed, tiny but definitely alive, on the warm towel.

"Hannah?" She jumped at the sound of her name.

"Lend a hand here?"

She sidled over to the operating table. "Lift her eyelid, okay?" Gingerly she did so. "Eyes rolled up or looking straight ahead?"

"Rolled up, I'd say," Hannah answered in a faint voice.

"All right, turn that knob one turn to the left. See it right there beside you? We want to let up on the anesthetic so she'll be coming out of it at just the right time. Here you go, Carrie, number three. And here's number four. Hannah? Grab a towel. How's yours doing, Zelda?"

"Great."

Hannah, towel in hand, felt the small moist body thrust into it.

"Clean its nose and mouth," he told her. "Then rub it with the towel—no, harder than that. You want to get it breathing properly. That looks good."

Hannah saw the small sides move in and out with regular breathing, and her own breath caught in wonderment.

"Okay, put it in the box. Uh-oh, one more. This one looks pretty runty. Carrie, keep track of the anesthetic. We want her awake as soon as I suture. Here, Hannah. Clean towel, we've got another one."

Hannah went to work on the puppy, feeling even through the enveloping towel that this one was smaller, less solid than the other. She cleaned it and rubbed it, but it lay pathetically inert in her hands.

"Hold it with its head down and give it a shake," he ordered. "No, harder than that. There. Breathing now?"

Hannah felt damp with perspiration, tense, anxious, as she massaged the tiny body and then at last saw the in-and-out movement of breath.

"Yes!" she cried. "Yes, he's breathing!"

Bent over the table, Jake glanced up at her for a fraction of a second, their eyes meeting. He gave a short nod of approval. "Good work," he said, and returned to what he was doing. Hannah took the smallest puppy to the box where Zelda crouched, examining the others.

"Oh, my," Zelda said with a frown. "He *is* a scrawny one, isn't he?"

"But he'll be all right, won't he?" Hannah said quickly.

Zelda gave a small shrug. "We'll see. It's up to his mother."

"You mean she might not—"

"Here we go," Jake interrupted, carrying the mother over to the box and gently placing her inside. "She's just waking up. We try to time it that way with a C-section so the minute I've closed she's ready to wake and look after the puppies."

And as Hannah watched, the puppies began to scramble against their mother. She opened her eyes, examined them and at once began licking them busily.

"How wonderful," Hannah breathed softly. Zelda got up and moved away. "I'd better tell Frank everything's fine," she said.

Hannah went on looking at the puppies, seeking out the runt she'd been holding. "That one's getting pushed away," she said. "Can't we help him—"

"Let his mother handle it," Jake said. "She knows best. Sometimes puny ones like that don't make it, that's all." He was studying Hannah intently, and now, looking up, she once more met his eyes. She felt weak with the excitement of it all. As a newspaper reporter she had been in exciting, even dangerous, situations before, but she'd never experienced anything quite like this. And there was something else, quite indefinable, that made her legs feel wobbly and unsure. His look seemed to go all the way through her, to her very core, a probing, assessing kind of look.

"Not bad for a city girl," he said softly. She looked down, away from the penetrating gaze. "And you're right," he added. "I don't know you as well as I thought I did."

She raised her eyes again to his, but now he was staring down at the silk pant legs of her jumpsuit, smudged and torn.

"I guess you'd better add that to the pile of dry cleaning I'm going to owe you." He grinned.

HANNAH WAS UP AND OUT early the next morning, following directions Zelda had given her to a store in the village. Within twenty minutes she was outside again, wearing a new sweatshirt, jeans and sneakers. In the packages she carried were cotton shirts and a denim skirt. She tossed them into the car, glancing ruefully at the two expensive outfits that lay on the seat, then looked around for the dry-cleaning shop Zelda had recommended. She located it across the street and walked over. A bell above the door tinkled as she entered.

"Mercy," said the small elderly woman behind the counter, looking at Hannah over her glasses and then at the pile of soiled clothes. "Those are a sight, aren't they? Well, we'll do our best. Staying with Zelda Miles, are you?"

"Yes. Just for a—a while," Hannah said, giving her name and hurrying back out. But when she had driven home and parked the car in Zelda's driveway, she didn't go directly into the house. Instead, she made her way eagerly along the path to the gap in the hedge. She was feeling, this morning, a strange elation, a sense that something important had happened. Twice she had wakened in the night thinking of what he'd said to her. *Not bad for a city girl.* Hannah's heart had jumped, hearing him say it, as if it was the highest praise. Not that it *mattered,* she hastened to remind herself. Not that it changed any of her plans. It was just that she'd been caught up in the small wonder of what they had done. No doubt it was old stuff to Jake McCabe, but to Hannah it was a revelation. She was eager to see the puppies this morning. Was she also eager to see Jake McCabe? A small distant voice asked the question, but Hannah refused to answer.

She went to the same side door they had used the night before, and knocked timidly. It was flung open almost at once, but not by Jake. A man in his sixties stood there, legs slightly bowed, stiff gray hair standing up in a long crew cut.

"Morning!" he said cordially.

"Good morning." Hannah could hear Jake's voice from somewhere inside—on the telephone, she thought. "I'm Hannah Chase. I'm staying next door with Mrs. Miles, and I—"

"Oh, *you're* the one," the man said as if everything was clear now. "My name's Tully. I help the doc out around the kennels and the surgery and so on. Retired coupla years ago—used to be a farmer. My son's took over now, but I can't abide sitting around, so I came to work here. Come on in, why don't you? Doc's on the phone, is all."

"I was wondering how the puppies were doing," Hannah said, stepping inside.

"Mitzi's pups?" he asked, grinning. "Oh, they're in fine shape. Be going home today or tomorrow. Here, I'll show you."

Hannah glanced across the office at Jake, who was scowling into the telephone. "When did it happen? . . . I see. That makes three this month, doesn't it . . . No, I'm pretty sure we can rule out brucellosis, but it's got me stumped. I just don't see... All right, I'll be out there as soon as I can make it."

He slammed the phone down, staring at it angrily for a moment. Then he seemed to become aware of her presence and turned to her. "Good morning." She thought he was making an effort to shift to a more cordial mood, and was half-embarrassed that she'd come at an awkward time. "Here to see the puppies? Tully'll show them to you. Tully!"

But the man was already opening the door to an adjoining room, which seemed to be a small laundry or washroom. "Moved 'em out of the kennels," he explained. "Mitzi didn't care for the noise. It's nice and quiet in here."

Hannah could hear yipping and barking from behind another door, and she sympathized with Mitzi. She glanced at Jake again. His face was still stern and thoughtful, but he said, "Go ahead. Mitzi enjoys showing them off." His thoughts were somewhere else, she could tell, and she felt vaguely let down. What had she expected, anyway? Some kind of special treatment? She moved into the little washroom and there on the floor was the box with Mitzi and the puppies. Mitzi lifted her head to see who was coming in, then at once looked back at the puppies as if to count them and make sure none was missing. Hannah knelt and stroked her head.

"You've found a more appropriate outfit, I see," Jake said behind her.

She kept her eyes on the dogs. "I thought it might be wise. In case any more emergencies come up." She watched the puppies nuzzling around their mother and noticed that the smallest one was off to one side and seemed weak and quiet.

"Why doesn't that little one nurse like the others?" she demanded, turning to look up at him.

"He's the runt and he probably won't make it. I told you that last night."

"But why doesn't his mother do something about it?"

"She's doing it. She's letting nature take care of it, which is the right way."

"You mean she's just going to let him—"

"No, no," he said with a trace of annoyance. "That's not the way it is. She's doing it *because* she's a good mother. She's protecting the others, seeing that they do well. She can't waste her strength on the one who probably won't live, anyway.''

"But you could save it—you could feed it and give it vitamins and whatever it needs!" Hannah protested, standing up angrily and confronting him.

"Oh, Lord, deliver me from sentimental women!" he exploded. "Do you realize I have to leave right now for a farm where a cow's just lost her calf—and it's the third one in a month on the same farm? I can't spare the time to coddle a runty pup when that farmer's worried to death he's going to lose his herd and possibly his farm. Loss of calves represents a real loss of investment to him, and he's looking to me for answers. If you're so damned worried about the puppy, *you* take care of it. I certainly don't have the time.''

He turned on his heel and strode out of the office, calling over his shoulder to Tully, "I'll be out at Rittenmyer's place. I'll try to get back by noon."

Tully waved him off, then joined Hannah. "Don't pay too much mind to him," he said awkwardly. "He don't mean to be so short-tempered. It's just that he's got this thing on his mind, trying to get to the bottom of it. When he can't seem to help it gets to him sometimes, and then he flies off the handle.''

"Well, yes, of course, I see," Hannah said, but to herself added that she did not see at all. It wasn't her fault about the cow losing its calf, and furthermore, the entire conversation about the puppy had seemed to her completely unfeeling, no matter how he explained it. More likely, she guessed, he was taking out his problems on her, and that was something she could do without. She looked back at the small inert body in the corner of the box and said with sudden decisiveness, "Do you think Dr. McCabe meant it when he said I could take care of the puppy? And what would the owner say?''

Tully's eyes squinted into a smile. ''Why sure Doc meant it. Wouldn't've said it otherwise. And Frank Goodwin, man who owns Mitzi, he wouldn't want the runt, anyway.'' He gave her a sharp look. ''Think you want to take it on? It's a real lot of work, you know—got to feed him every hour or so round the clock, keep him warm.''

''I can do that,'' Hannah said firmly. ''I've got plenty of time.'' Deliberately she avoided thinking about the series of articles she had come here to write, the bait that Bob Anderson had used to lure her to Harrison Falls in the first place. ''I'm sure I can save him. What do I need, Tully?''

A quarter of an hour later she left the office bearing the puppy in a small basket over her arm. In the other hand she held a shopping bag with puppy formula, vitamins and a tiny baby bottle, which Tully had had to search for. ''I just know there's one here someplace— Carrie used to use it for her dolls,'' he had said. And at the door he had wished her luck.

Walking carefully along the path toward Zelda's house, peeking now and again at the small towel-wrapped bundle in the basket, Hannah tried to contain the anger that welled up whenever she recalled the scene with Jake McCabe. *Sentimental women* indeed! Of all the insulting, thoughtless things to say. And the night before she'd been so sure he approved of her. *Not bad for a city girl,* he had said, and she'd thought he meant it as praise. But how idiotic of her to take it to heart that way! To be pleased that he approved of her—to come running over the very next morning expecting the mood of the night before to still be there. Well, there was cer-

tainly no need to have anything more to do with him.
Rapidly Hannah began making plans. She would set up
her computer in her room, keeping the puppy there so
that she could keep an eye on him and feed him whenever he was hungry. Then she'd work on the notes she
had stored in the computer, put them in some kind of
order so she could start an outline for her piece on local
politics. It would work out just fine and keep her busy
enough so there'd be no need for her to have anything
further to do with any of the inhabitants of Harrison
Falls. They were very fine respectable people, no doubt,
but they were distracting, and she had no desire to get
involved in their lives. For a moment the contradiction
in her plan occurred to her. Writing a story about a small
town's politics and not getting acquainted with its citizens certainly showed very little logic. Well, then, she
would think of another subject to write about, that was
all.

"What in the world!" Zelda Miles said, coming to the
door as Hannah climbed the stairs to the porch. Zelda
was in her jeans and apron again, a large spoon in her
hand. "If I didn't know better, I'd think there was a
puppy in that basket."

"It's the runty one," Hannah explained. "He just
wasn't going to make it, Zelda, and I couldn't stand that.
Dr. McCabe said I could try to save him, and Tully gave
me the right things."

Zelda peered into the basket. "He certainly doesn't
look too hearty, does he? Well, who knows? It's worth
a try."

Hannah was relieved that Zelda made no objection.
"I'll keep him in my room," she said hastily. "I
wouldn't want him to be underfoot or anything. And I'll

be right there to feed him. Tully says he'll need something every hour or so.''

But Zelda was already leading the way into the big old-fashioned kitchen. ''Shoot, I think you'd better keep him in here,'' she said reasonably. ''We'll make up a bed for him and keep an eye on him.''

''Oh, but I don't want to put you out—'' Hannah started to object, but Zelda interrupted.

''Look at it this way,'' she said, waving the spoon. ''If you were a forlorn little mutt like that, where would you rather be—stuck up in a bedroom away from everything, or right in the middle of things where people were coming and going all the time and you felt like you were part of the family? Kitchen's where he belongs.''

It was such a homey, kindhearted bit of reasoning that Hannah had to laugh, and some of her angry mood began to dissipate as she and Zelda assembled a bed and prepared the puppy's first bottle of formula. When at last she was seated at the kitchen table, holding the puppy and trying to interest him in eating, she said hesitantly, ''I think Dr. McCabe—Jake—thinks I'm crazy wanting to save this little runt. He was all upset about some cow problems and wouldn't even discuss it.'' She nodded toward the tiny animal in her arms.

Zelda returned to the pot of soup that was simmering on the stove. She gave it a stir, then put her spoon down. ''Is that so? Well, we'll just have to show him a thing or two, won't we?'' Hannah kept her eyes on the puppy as he finally connected with the bottle and began sucking, but all the time she could feel Zelda's eyes on her, scrutinizing her curiously.

What on earth am I doing? The thought struck Hannah as she sat there in the warm country kitchen. *I've never even had a pet before. And what about the fu-*

*ture? What about when he's no longer a tiny bundle in
a basket?* She took a deep breath and closed the door
firmly on all the ''what ifs.'' The future would take care
of itself, she decided. It was, for her, not a characteris-
tic decision and she knew it. Somehow, here in Harrison Falls, all the rules were changed. It didn't seem to
matter.

MORE THAN ONCE during the next twenty-four hours
Hannah wondered what had ever made her think she was
equipped to deal with an underweight lethargic puppy
with an eating problem. She insisted on carrying him
upstairs in his basket at night, along with a thermos of
formula, so that Zelda wouldn't be disturbed. But waking every hour or more to try to coax him to eat resulted
in almost no sleep at all for her. Daylight found her no
more rested than she'd been when she went to bed, and
still the puppy had taken only a little nourishment.
Hannah rubbed smarting eyes and reminded herself that
it wasn't any worse than when she'd stayed up all night
waiting for a jury to come in when she was covering a
trial. Then she swung her legs over the side of the bed
and went wearily to the basket. This time the puppy
surprised her by whining audibly. And when she offered him the tiny bottle, he attacked it eagerly, drain-
ing it.

''I think we should call him Samson,'' she told Zelda
happily when she carried him down to the kitchen. Zelda
was already at the stove turning out a stack of pancakes. She filled a heavy white mug with coffee for
Hannah and peeked approvingly into the basket.

''Sounds like a good name to me. Maybe he'll grow
into it. Hello there, Samson. Sam, I'm going to call you.
More your size.''

Hannah sipped the hot fresh coffee. "Oh, that's delicious, Zelda. I really needed a pick-me-up this morning."

"Not too much sleep, I'll bet."

"Not a whole lot, no."

"Pancakes are ready. Maybe after you eat you can grab another forty winks."

Hannah watched Zelda removing them from the griddle, golden brown and fragrant.

"Oh, just coffee will be fine for me, thanks," she said.

"Nonsense. These are whole wheat. Besides, you don't get any mileage at all out of a cup of coffee. Here, dig in. How about some of Carrie's honey on top?"

Hannah laughed weakly and sat back in her chair. "Well, maybe just one."

Zelda filled plates for both of them and sat opposite her.

"I'll be going out with Carrie after breakfast," the woman said.

"Goodness, is it Saturday already?" Hannah realized that she'd lost track of time and distance here. She felt several thousand miles from New York rather than a mere 250, and the days of the week had no meaning whatsoever. A small stab of guilt nudged her at the thought of the portable computer in her bedroom upstairs. Oh, well, she'd get to work before long. Just as soon as she'd rested up a bit and the puppy was stronger....

"Yep. We ought to get in a pretty good day's work. Finish medicating the hives, so we'll be ready when the new queens come."

"It's good of you to help her, Zelda."

Zelda glanced at her. "Shoot, I'm the one being helped. I was always so busy. Then Fred died—my husband. And my kids live far away. No, Carrie's been real good for me.''

''I'm sure you've been good for her, too.''

''Well, one hand washes the other,'' Zelda said practically. Then, more briskly, ''Look here, out on the porch is a good big lounger you could fall asleep in easy. Take Sam out there with you and just relax this morning.''

''Maybe I will.''

''And if I'm not back by noon, dig into the refrigerator and help yourself.''

Hannah glanced down at her plate and realized she had eaten three pancakes. ''Goodness, I don't think I'll be hungry again before Labor Day.''

''Sure you will. Besides, you could use a pound or two. People in the city don't know how to eat.''

Hannah shook her head, laughing. She had a second cup of coffee after Zelda had driven off in a rusty old pickup truck. Then, making sure the puppy was still asleep, she took a quick bath and dressed in her jeans and one of her new T-shirts. Samson was stirring when she returned to him. She mixed a fresh batch of formula, warmed it and put it in the thermos, then carried basket and thermos out to the porch. She saw the wicker chaise longue Zelda had recommended, but the morning was cool and the wooden steps, with the sun shining on them, looked more inviting. She sat on the top step, lifted the squirming puppy out and offered him the bottle. He sought it eagerly and began sucking on it at once. Hannah no longer felt tired, but limp and relaxed. Her shoulder-length dark hair was hanging loose. Somehow it seemed a nuisance here to bother with hot rollers and hairdos. And the plans she'd made, ages ago, it seemed, to go out hunting for a new place to stay, were no longer important. She liked Zelda Miles, and she was feeling at home in the big old house. All she had to do was mind her own business and avoid Jake McCabe. A temperamental man like him was the last thing she needed in her life now.

"Good morning." The voice was so close it made her start. She looked up to see Jake McCabe standing there, one foot on the bottom step, smiling at her. She looked back quickly at the puppy in her lap. "Good morning," she said coolly.

"I came over to apologize," he said. "May I get that out of the way first?"

She raised her head more slowly this time, studying him openly. He was in a faded blue denim shirt and his usual jeans. His sandy hair fell over his forehead in a rumpled way. She suspected it often did that. She could see the smile lines at the corners of his eyes.

Her shoulders sketched a faint shrug. "Okay. Suit yourself."

"Well, then, I apologize. For being rude yesterday. No excuse for it—except that I *was* worried, and had things on my mind."

She looked away again, but she could feel his eyes on her as she sat there feeding the puppy.

"All right. Apology accepted," she said.

"You seem to be doing very well with him," he said. "I guess I was wrong about that, too, wasn't I?"

She gave him a sly glance. "You'd be surprised what a sentimental woman can do when her mind's made up."

"Oops. I apologize again. Did you have a rough night?"

"Fairly. But things seem better this morning."

"I'd say so," he said, his eyes still on her. "Anyway, I had another reason for coming over here. I wanted to ask you to take a ride with me this morning."

"Take a ride with you where?" She felt a sudden leaping of her heart that surprised her, coming so unexpectedly. Really, she must get better control of her emotions, she scolded herself.

"Out on calls. Just two or three stops, but it would be a chance for you to see some of the country around here. And there's something special I want to show you."

"What?"

"Wait and see. Will you come?"

"What about Samson?"

"Samson!"

"Well, I think it's going to be Sam, actually." She asked anxiously, "It is all right for me to keep him, isn't it? Tully seemed to think so, but—"

"It's fine. I talked to Frank—the owner—last night and explained. He's grateful for your help and you're welcome to the puppy. Bring him along in his basket."

"He'll be all right?"

"If he isn't, he has his personal physician handy."

Hannah laughed and tossed her head back so that her hair rippled across her shoulders. "I'm taking your word for all this," she said. "But you'll have to give me a minute to pack him up. Clean towels and formula, and I have to rinse his bottle."

"Nobody ever said motherhood was easy," he said, still grinning.

Hannah hurried inside to get ready, the pounding of her heart loud in her ears. Well, after all, it was only sensible to get acquainted with the area where one was vacationing, wasn't it? And if she was going to write her series on grass-roots political activity, what better way to get local color than to meet some of the people here? Except that the image that kept recurring was not of the careful notes stored in her computer, but of Jake Mc-Cabe's long lean body and strong brown hands, and the idea of sitting next to him in the Jeep Cherokee waiting in front of his house.

She hurried up to her room to dab on a touch of lip-stick and to swipe at her hair with a brush, then went to the kitchen to wash Sam's bottle.

"Ready," she said, reappearing on the porch.

For a moment his eyes traveled over her, taking in the slim waist, the curves, the long legs, the brushed hair struck by morning sun.

"Ready," he agreed, and picked up the basket.

CHAPTER THREE

"WELL, WHAT DO YOU think of it?" He glanced sideways at her as they headed away from the village, the bright spring morning unfolding around them. New green was on all the trees, and the white blossoms of dogwoods showed in drifts against it.

"Think of what?"

"The country, the day, the world in general."

Hannah, sitting with the puppy's basket on her lap, looked around her. "It's beautiful, I have to admit."

"Difficult admission for a city girl to make, is that it?"

She laughed. "Well, it doesn't change my mind, if that's what you mean. I certainly wouldn't dream of living anywhere but the city."

"Why not?" He made a skillful turn at a crossroad and headed the Jeep onto a narrower, high-crowned county road.

"Oh...well, goodness, it's where I've always lived. It's where my work is. Besides, I don't really belong in the country. I don't...understand it, exactly."

"Mmm. I'm not sure that's an argument. But I guess I know what you're saying."

"Have you always lived here in Harrison Falls?"

"Yes, except for going to Cornell."

"Always knew you wanted to be a vet?"

"Just about always."

"It's nice when you know," she said. She tried, briefly, to imagine him in a big city, but the picture refused to appear.

"What about you? Where did you grow up?"

"In New York City. Long Island, too. Went to school all over the place, including Europe."

"But didn't you always know you wanted to write?"

Hannah thought back, remembering lonely days with a succession of nannies, lonely summers in her grandfather's big house near the sea, and a small Hannah busy with pencil and paper creating a world of her own.

"Well, now that you mention it, yes, I guess I did." The conversation seemed to be crowding uncomfortably close. She brushed her windblown hair back from her face and changed the subject. "Where are we going?"

He glanced at her, a quick look that took in the flying hair, the hand curved over the sleeping puppy. Then hastily he returned his attention to the car, edging over to the side of the road as a pickup truck approached from the other direction. The driver, a man in overalls, waved and Jake waved back.

"First stop is Rittenmyer's farm. He's the man who lost those calves. He has another cow due and I want to see if she's all right. Would you like to put that basket on the back seat?"

Hannah glanced around. The back seat was already fairly full with boxes, cartons, boots, equipment of all sorts.

"Sam's fine like this," she said. "I want to be sure he doesn't get cold. Are there more stops after that?"

"Only one or two. I have to get to the post office before it closes at noon. Carrie's bees arrived and she won't want them to stay in their packing box all weekend.

Neither will the postmaster. And I have office hours this afternoon. Here we go.''

He turned into a lane leading to a white farmhouse, modest-looking but with well-kept barns and outbuildings. A woman came out to greet them, tucking back her hair and wiping her hands on her jeans.

"Oh, Jake, I'm real glad you got here."

"Hi, Thelma. This is a friend, Hannah Chase."

"How do you do." The woman managed a small nervous smile. "Jake, we can't find Blossom—she's gone off somewhere. Harv thinks she wants to have her calf by herself."

"Well, they do that, you know."

"Yes, but all the bad luck we've had lately..."

"Which way did Harv go?"

She pointed. "Off toward the north field, that way. He thinks she's probably had it by now."

"Well, look, why don't I try the other direction? Hannah, you want to wait here?"

"Can't I come?" she asked.

"Sure. The pup can stay in the Jeep."

"Oh, look at that, will you?" Thelma was momentarily distracted by the sight of Samson in his basket. "Don't worry, I'll keep an eye on him. If that isn't the cutest..."

Hannah put the basket down carefully on the seat, thanking Thelma, then hurried after Jake, who had grabbed a rope and was already striding ahead, out past the house and up a long sloping field. "If I was a cow I think I'd like the looks of all these low bushes," he was saying as she caught up with him. "She'll probably try to hide the calf if she's had it already."

"Is that what they do?"

"Sometimes."

She shaded her eyes and looked far ahead, up where the field rose more steeply and where a herd of black-and-white cattle grazed in the new grass.

"Are those beef or dairy cattle?" she asked.

He stared at her, then smiled his wide, quick smile. "There speaks a city girl for sure. This is a dairy farm and those are milk cows."

Hannah blushed furiously. "Oh. I didn't notice." She was beginning to breathe rapidly and wondered why the climb seemed to be using muscles she hadn't been aware of in her aerobics class.

They came to a small stream winding down through the meadow. Jake stepped across it easily and turned to give her a hand. His touch was strong and sure, and Hannah felt the smallness of her hand in his. Her knees were all at once unsure and weak. He smiled at her again.

"Why don't you wait here?" he said. "I'll go the rest of the way—she might have climbed pretty high."

"I'm perfectly all right," she insisted.

"No, it would be a good idea, really. Sit here and keep your eyes open. You might see something that'll help."

The sun was beating down strongly now, and Hannah had no desire to slow him down or become an encumbrance.

"All right." She watched as he strode off with long strides, bending his muscular frame slightly against the slope. Then she sank to the ground near the little stream, pulling her knees to her chin and wrapping her arms around them.

She had told Jake McCabe she could never live anywhere except a city, yet there was a quality about this bright fresh morning that Hannah had to admit no city could offer. Was there perhaps another side of her that had yet to be awakened? An awareness of a different kind of beauty and, yes, an excitement? Hannah thought about it, but her thoughts kept straying to the tall man striding across the hilly field, and no matter how she tried to concentrate, it was his face that kept stealing into her mind. She sighed, slid her legs down and leaned back with her elbows on the ground behind her, propping herself up. She turned toward a low bush that was sheltering her from the sun. There, staring out at her, not three feet away, were two large brown eyes.

Hannah screamed.

She leapt to her feet, and almost at the same moment saw Jake whirl around and look back at her. Then he dropped his rope and came plunging down the slope toward her, reaching her in seconds and wrapping her in his arms, holding her so close that her own pounding heartbeat seemed to mingle with his.

"Hannah, what is it? Hannah—are you all right?" His cheek was against her hair. She could smell the outdoors on him, the sun and the wind, along with a sensual male essence that made her dizzy with a strange unfamiliar longing. She wanted to stay forever in this strong embrace, safe and cared for.

"I'm all right," she murmured.

"But what happened? What is it?" He pulled away from her, holding her by the shoulders and peering into her face anxiously.

"It's—there's something—right there," she said tremulously, pointing toward the bush.

He dropped to his haunches and looked, parting the low branches carefully, then getting to his feet again, his face showing an obvious effort to hold back laughter. Finally he exploded with it, a hearty laugh that was so infectious Hannah couldn't help joining in.

"Is that it?" she asked. "Did I find the calf?"

"You did, and I guarantee it's not dangerous. Better still, from here it looks healthy. Hannah, you brought me luck today." And suddenly he bent down, tipped up her chin with one hand and kissed her, a warm spontaneous kiss that deepened as his arms encircled her and held her close, pressing her against him. To her surprise, Hannah found her own arms around his neck, her hands touching the back of his head where the sandy hair grew thick. Her passion roused, she kissed him back, forgetful of time and place and the strangeness of the situation.

Slowly they drew apart, still staring into one another's eyes. Hannah swallowed and said hesitantly, "Shouldn't we—I mean, don't we have to do something about this? You know, bring the calf back, or..."

He put a hand up and stroked her hair tenderly, keeping his eyes on her face for a long moment. "I wish we didn't," he murmured. "I wish we had all day out here, just the two of us...." Then he took a deep breath and seemed to return to the present.

"Stay here a minute," he said. "I think I spotted Blossom farther up the hill. I'll bring her back and we'll lead her home. The calf will follow her."

She nodded and watched him go up the hill again. Then she knelt down and looked at the calf under the bush, unafraid this time, parting the branches carefully for a better view. The large liquid eyes stared back at her, and Hannah reached in, touching the soft nose gently.

In moments Jake was back, leading a black-and-white cow who plodded along amiably chewing her cud and showing no remorse for the anxiety she had caused everyone.

"Can you hold her for a minute?" Jake asked. "She's unusually gentle for a holstein. Some of them aren't. I'll get the calf on its feet and it'll tag along, I'm sure."

He carefully pulled the calf from its hiding place and set it on its feet.

"A little heifer," he said, and then gave her a twinkling look. "That's a girl, you know."

"I know *that* much," she said with mock indignation.

"And as far as I can see, a healthy one. Harv's going to be pleased at that. All right, I'll take the lead rope now, and we'll head back."

The calf did its best to totter after its mother, but halfway there Jake handed Hannah the rope. "Here. Think you can lead Blossom? This calf needs some help."

Hannah took the rope and Jake leaned over, picked up the calf and carried it the rest of the way.

Harv Rittenmyer, a burly man with weathered features, smiled from ear to ear at the sight of the procession, and his wife, Thelma, grew teary with relief.

"Hannah did it," Jake said at once. "She's the one who found the calf."

"Only by accident," Hannah insisted, but both Rittenmyers congratulated her and invited the two of them inside for coffee.

"Better be on our way," Jake said. "Have to be back for office hours, and we still have a couple of stops to make."

Later in the Jeep he explained, "At the next stop they're going to *insist* on giving us coffee. I figured we'd better save ourselves for that."

Hannah, feeling suddenly shy at being alone with him again, was silent for a few minutes while they made their way onto the county road again. At last she said, "You know...what happened back there, well, I wouldn't want you to get the wrong idea."

He glanced at her, not really taking her seriously, she thought.

"What would the wrong idea be?"

"What I mean is, I want you to understand that I make it a policy not to form...attachments."

"Never?" His eyebrows went up.

"Well...no. I've had a lot of male friends. I still do. But not serious love affairs. I find it works better for me. For my life, that is."

"You really do like to plan things, don't you?"

She decided that he still wasn't taking her seriously. "I just wanted you to understand," she said a little primly.

"Oh, I do," he said. "Only couldn't we just think of it as a kind of celebration?"

"What do you mean, a celebration?"

"Well, of a nice day in the country, say."

She gave him a suspicious look. "I suppose so."

He went on driving, a half smile on his face, and in the basket the puppy began to stir and struggle. Hannah offered him his bottle and they rode on in silence.

The Reeds' farm didn't have the prosperous tidy look of the Rittenmyers'. As they drove in, Hannah could see that the house was unpainted and shabby, although a huge rosebush loaded with buds climbed one side and rioted over the low roof. In the yard was a rusty pickup and, sitting on concrete blocks, a car of ancient vintage, missing all its tires and one door. Beyond the house, a line of washing blew in the breeze, and chickens pecked around the front steps.

"What's the errand here?" Hannah whispered as they parked.

He got out and reached into the back seat, picking up a heavy cardboard box shaped like a carrying case. "Have to make a delivery."

A man, woman and a little girl of five or so were on the porch ready to greet them before they even reached the house.

"Hello, Bob, Nettie. Hi, Melissa."

"Well, morning, Jake. Didn't expect you today," Bob Reed said. He was a tall thin man in bib overalls. His wife, a foot shorter, was a round little woman in slacks and an apron.

"But we're just real glad to see you," she said warmly.

"This is Hannah Chase, a friend of mine," Jake said, and Nettie Reed gave her a broad smile.

"Now just come right on in, both of you," she said. "Melissa, say how do you do to Dr. McCabe and the lady."

Melissa's finger slid into her mouth. "Hi," she whispered.

Hannah leaned over and asked her, "Would you like to see something nice?"

The little girl nodded vigorously.

"All right. Come and look." Hannah took her free hand and led her over to the Jeep, where the puppy lay sleeping in his basket on the front seat. Melissa's eyes grew round and wide.

"Can I touch him?" she breathed.

"Yes, of course. Only very gently. He's a tiny baby."

The small hand came out and stroked the puppy, who stretched his hind legs but didn't wake up.

"Is he yours?"

"He...seems to be, yes."

"I had a kitty."

Hannah caught the past tense and asked cautiously, "Has he gone away?"

The little girl nodded. "He went to heaven."

"Oh, dear. I'm sorry to hear that."

"Me, too."

"Well, don't be too sorry until you see what I brought," said Jake's voice behind them, and both turned to see him standing there against the morning sunlight. He set the box he'd been carrying on the ground and raised its lid. A half-grown kitten, tiger-striped with a pure white chest, sat blinking up at them. Melissa's breath caught in wonderment.

"Whose is that?" she asked cautiously.

"Belongs to Melissa Reed," Jake answered, lifting the kitten out and handing it to her. The little girl's features were alight with rapture as she held it close. Her parents moved in to see the new arrival.

"Oh, Doc, what a nice thing to do," Nettie Reed said, shaking her head with a happy smile. "I can't tell you how that child's been moping since old Winky died."

"I thought as much," Jake said. "This one should make a good pet. She's been spayed, had all her shots—"

"Oh, mercy, just think of that. Bob, isn't that just the kindest thing!"

Bob Reed cleared his throat. "Sure do appreciate it, Doc."

Jake waved away their thanks and turned to Melissa. "Now, be sure to take good care of her and no squeezing her around the middle. Give her a chance to exercise and grow up."

"What will you name her?" Hannah asked.

"Winky," the child said promptly.

"If you've got a good thing, why change it?" Jake smiled at Melissa and mussed her hair. Over the top of the little girl's head, Hannah caught his glance. She felt a sudden tremor of emotion and looked away.

"Now come on," Nettie said firmly. "I just put a pot of coffee on, and my blueberry muffins must be ready to come out of the oven."

They all crowded into the little house and settled themselves around a big wooden table that took up most of the kitchen. Jake and Bob Reed talked about farm conditions, the weather, the economy, while Nettie kept up a steady stream of friendly conversation that seemed to demand no particular response from Hannah. It amazed Hannah to find how easily she seemed to fit in, how much at home she felt here. A secret pleasure at this unexpected recognition warmed her as much as Nettie Reed's coffee. In a chair at the table, but actually in a world of her own, Melissa sat stroking the kitten, who seemed pleased with all the attention. Cups were filled with steaming fresh coffee, and fragrant muffins were piled on a plate and urged on everyone. It was a long half hour before Jake and Hannah could manage to break away.

"What a wonderful family," Hannah said spontaneously when they were back in the Jeep and pulling out of the lane. On the rickety porch all the Reeds were waving them off.

"They are, aren't they?" he agreed, swinging onto the road. "Not the most prosperous, perhaps—Bob never did seem able to manage much more than one cow and a cornfield. Nettie works on the line at Harrison Electrical, the factory on the other side of town, and that helps out. But they have each other, and Melissa. That seems to be enough for them."

"Then I'd say they were lucky," Hannah murmured.

"I would, too. But the little girl really has been grieving for her cat. It got hit by a car a couple of weeks ago and I couldn't save it."

She looked at his lean profile as he drove, trying to figure out the contradictions she saw in him. Certainly he had seemed short-tempered and indifferent when she'd urged him to try to save the puppy. Yet he had taken considerable time and effort to make little Melissa Reed happy. Did she, herself, perhaps rub him the wrong way? Had he seen her as an overbearing career woman making unreasonable demands? Yet back in the meadow when he'd held her close to him and kissed her... The memory made Hannah swallow suddenly and a tremor of reaction stirred in her. No, that was only a thing of the moment. A situation that had thrown them together...

He glanced at her, almost as if he'd been having similar thoughts of his own. "Are you up to one more stop?"

"Of course."

"This is the thing I really wanted to show you."

He pulled in at another farm with a neat white house and prosperous-looking barns and sheds. It resembled their first stop, the Rittenmyers', yet Hannah was beginning to see that in spite of similarities, each farm was distinctive. This one, for example, had an enormous vegetable garden, which seemed to be thriving with early lettuce and young tomato plants.

Jake followed her look. "Tom and Ruth Winfield's place. That garden's Ruthie's. It's quite a sight later in the summer. She plants flowers in between the rows of vegetables. Ah. Here comes Tom."

Tom Winfield was a middle-aged farmer with sunsquinting eyes and a wide smile. He shook both their hands and said Ruthie'd be real sorry to have missed them, but she'd driven into the village on some errands, she and their daughter.

"Can't stay, anyway, Tom," Jake said. "Just wanted to see how the new horse was doing today. And I wanted to show Hannah the little mare, if that's all right."

"Oh, you bet. Come on. They're both in the stable. I was just going to turn 'em out into the field. The new one's doing fine now—seems to be over whatever it was that got to her yesterday."

"Tom bought his daughter a new horse to ride," Jake explained to Hannah. "And it colicked yesterday. They do that sometimes when there's a change of feed, or even water."

"Oh." Hannah had no idea what kind of complaint he was describing, but she nodded politely as Tom Winfield led them to a small neat stable with two stalls. In one was a sleek brown horse with a long elegant neck and sensitive ears, which twitched as they approached. Jake opened the stall, went in and ran his hands over the horse, glanced into the feed box in one corner and nodded approvingly. "Looks fine today, you're right," he said. Then he indicated the next stall. "Look here," he said to Hannah.

Hannah moved closer and saw a slightly smaller horse, a chestnut mare with flaxen mane and tail and a white blaze down her face.

"Isn't she a beauty?" Jake said.

Even Hannah's untutored city eyes could see that she was. "Oh, how lovely," she breathed.

"Couldn't ask for a better horse," Tom Winfield said behind them. "Barb, my daughter, learned to ride on her, and she's always been gentle as a lamb. Now Barb thinks she's ready for something a little livelier. That's why we got the new one here.''

"And Tom's agreed to sell me Foxfire—as a birthday present for Carrie."

"What a wonderful idea!" The little mare thrust her head over the railing and Hannah stroked her forehead where the white blaze started.

"The selling part was Jake's idea," Tom Winfield said with a shake of his head. "All the favors this fellow's done for us, I wanted to give him the horse, but he wouldn't sit still for that."

"Certainly not," Jake said curtly. "And she's worth a good deal more than I'm paying. A gentle horse like that—she'll be just right for Carrie. Only not a word now," he cautioned Hannah suddenly. "Her birthday's still two weeks away."

"I won't say a thing," Hannah promised. "But what a thrill for her!"

"There'll be a party," Jake added. "You and Zelda are both invited, of course."

"Thank you," she said in a small voice. Once again she felt a curious warmth at the way she seemed to fit in here. How easy and familiar it all was!

They lingered for another few minutes in the stable, then explained to Tom Winfield that they had to return to town. Back in the Jeep, Hannah shifted the puppy's basket to a more comfortable position on her lap and glanced up at Jake.

"I'd say Carrie was pretty lucky to have a father like you," she said frankly.

His eyebrows went up as he glanced at her. "I've always thought I was the lucky one to have her."

"Oh, of course. She's lovely." Hannah hesitated, then asked, "Why doesn't she live with her mother?"

He negotiated a pothole in the road before answering. "Because her mother didn't want her," he said bluntly. "She wanted her career. She's a fashion designer, you see. All those trips to Hong Kong, Europe—well, they didn't leave much time for being a mother. Carrie would have been in the way." He gave her another sideways look and after a moment said, "You don't seem particularly shocked."

"Why should I be?" Hannah replied. "No one wanted me, either." The moment the words were out, she was surprised at herself. *I've never told anyone that before,* she thought with a sense of wonder.

"Is that really true?" He kept his eyes on the road ahead.

"Yes. I was in my mother's custody, but I went through a long list of nannies. Vacations, I was often at my grandparents' summer place on Long Island. Only it wasn't exactly what I—well, at least there was a household staff there. Sometimes the cook or the houseman would turn out to be friendly."

"You must know a thing or two about loneliness," he said in a quiet voice.

"Oh, well, we all have something, don't we?" Hannah said in a voice she tried to make light and uncaring.

"And now you're a little nervous about getting too close to anybody for fear of being hurt or left alone again—"

"Please!" she exploded. "Spare me the instant analysis. I'm just fine, Dr. McCabe. Please don't worry about me."

Taking one hand from the wheel, he reached out and put it over hers, resting on the edge of the basket. His hand was well-shaped and strong, Hannah noticed, and its touch was capable. For some reason tears began to sting her eyes. She pulled her own hand firmly away.

"Tell me about these bees we're going to pick up," she said.

The Harrison Falls Post Office occupied the other half of the building where Hannah had gone to buy her jeans and T-shirts. They parked in front, angling into one of the diagonal spaces alongside an elegant low sports car.

"Come on in," he said. "I'll introduce you to the postmaster."

"I'd better stay here and keep an eye on the puppy."

"Bring him along."

"Oh, well...all right."

The post-office lobby was one small room, empty now, with a high desk for customers' use and a counter behind which Hannah could see walls with slotted cubicles for mail.

"Morning, Ed," Jake said to the man behind the counter. "This is a visitor to town, Miss Hannah Chase. Staying out at Zelda's place. Ed Gretch, Hannah."

The postmaster was a small thin man with reading glasses on a cord around his neck. He greeted Hannah politely, then said to Jake, "I sure was worried you might not get here before closing, Jake. These damn bees—excuse me, ma'am—they had me worried what to do with them if you didn't show up. Well, I'd've brought 'em out to you, I reckon, but I'm just as glad I don't have to. Make me nervous."

"Absolutely harmless, Ed. No way they can get out of that case."

They watched as the man turned and picked up a narrow package, surrounded by a layer of thin screening, and placed it gingerly on the counter. They could hear an angry buzzing from inside the box.

"They sound healthy, anyway," Jake remarked, picking it up. "Much obliged, Ed." He turned to leave just as the outside door opened again and a man and a woman entered.

"Jake McCabe!" The woman's voice was high and clear, and Hannah stared curiously as the two came in from the bright sunlight. Both of them were young—light-haired and slender, casually dressed. The woman was wearing jodhpurs and riding boots, a honey-colored cashmere sweater knotted loosely around her neck. Sunglasses rested on top of her head, and her blond hair was caught back in a braid. "And here I've been trying to reach you on the telephone all morning!" She laughed.

The man with her was carrying several packages. "I've been pressed into service, as you see." He grinned. "Strictly for packhorse duty." He had an open, boyish face, his hair stylishly rumpled. He wore jeans, a denim shirt, Top-siders with no socks. Ralph Lauren every inch of the way, Hannah thought, recognizing a designer outfit when she saw one.

"Well, here I am," Jake said easily. "What can I do for you?"

The woman's eyes moved lightly to Hannah, taking in the basket with the puppy. Hannah could feel the stiffness of her new jeans, the windblown tangle of her hair, the touch of sunburn she was sure she had.

"I don't believe I've met your new assistant," the woman said.

Jake laughed loudly. "Oh, Lord, sorry. This isn't my assistant, Les. It's Miss Hannah Chase from New York City. And she's a very important newspaper writer, so we all have to watch what we say around her. Hannah, this is Leslie Harte. And that overburdened fellow there is her brother, Walker Harrison."

Leslie Harte's face grew faintly pink, but Hannah suspected she was not really abashed by her mistake. Hannah had an instant's impression that it would take a great deal more than that to disconcert her.

"How do you do," Hannah said.

"Oh, goodness, do forgive me," Leslie Harte fluted sweetly. "But what in the world is a New York newspaper person doing in Harrison Falls?"

"Just vacationing," Hannah answered in a level voice. But Walker Harrison was already letting his packages slide to the floor and stepping forward to take her hand.

"Well, New York's loss is definitely our gain," he said, smiling a crinkly, boyish smile at her. "Where are you staying?"

"With Mrs. Zelda Miles," she answered.

"Ah, yes. And that's how you happened to run into the good doctor here. I see it all now." He glanced at the sleeping puppy in the basket. "What's this he's palmed off on you? You'd better watch this fellow, Hannah. He can pull rabbits out of hats—or puppies, for that matter—and before you know it, you're hooked."

It was impossible not to respond to the man's friendliness. Hannah laughed and said, "I'm afraid he's not guilty this time, though. I volunteered."

"Jake, darling," Leslie Harte interrupted. "I've been wanting to get hold of you so I could remind you about the thing at our house next weekend. You know, I told you about it ages ago, but I was afraid you might have forgotten."

"Thing?" Jake's face creased in a frown.

"Oh, you know. The hunt club party. Well, it won't be exactly a party, but it's not a show, either. Oh, there'll be some judging—just for fun. Mostly for the kids and their ponies. That's why we need you. And also, it never hurts to have a vet around."

"Sure, I ought to be able to make it," he said.

"Wonderful. Look, I came in here to buy stamps. Let me do that before Mr. Gretch closes up. Come over here and I'll tell you more about the party. What in the world do you have there—bees?" She took his arm and led him to the window, and while the postmaster counted out stamps for her, she moved closer to Jake, holding his arm and pressing against him, her face upturned to his, talking with a low intimacy that seemed to indicate long familiarity.

Walker Harrison followed Hannah's look. "Old friends," he said, grinning. "Hey, are you going to be around this place for a while?"

"A few weeks, maybe."

"Wonderful!" He seemed genuinely pleased. "Then by all means come to the party next weekend. We'd love to have you. In fact, let me pick you up and bring you there. How about it?"

"Well, I don't know. I do have my own car—"

"Oh, but you're a guest. We wouldn't hear of it."

"And of course I'll have to arrange for a baby-sitter."

His eyebrows shot up in obvious surprise until she motioned with a nod toward Samson, snoozing blissfully on his towel. Then he broke into hearty laughter. "Let me know if you have any trouble with that," he told her. "I'll think of something."

Leslie Harte and Jake rejoined them, and Walker Harrison said, "I've just talked Hannah into it. She's coming to the party, too, and I've promised to see that she gets there.''

Hannah glanced at Leslie's face, expecting a glimmer of irritation. *Something about me has rubbed her the wrong way,* Hannah thought. *A woman can tell. Maybe seeing me with Jake? Perhaps she considers him her property.* But surprisingly, Leslie looked pleased. She smiled first at her brother, then at Hannah, saying, "Why, what a nice idea, Walker. Yes, do come, by all means, Hannah.''

"Thank you," Hannah murmured, still unconvinced. There was something behind Leslie's cordiality that she couldn't read.

"WE'VE ALL KNOWN the Harrisons forever," Jake explained as they drove home. "Their great-great-grandfather founded the town and their dad started the Harrison plant, which supports a lot of the people here. Makes electrical parts.''

Hannah nodded. "They seem pleasant," she said noncommittally.

"Oh, they're okay. Leslie's divorced. She came back here to live in her father's house when he retired. She's got a daughter about Carrie's age. Walker's taken over the factory management. Not married yet, but Zelda says every girl in town's after him.''

"I see." And she did, Hannah thought. Saw, too, why Leslie didn't mind Walker's inviting her to the party at their house. Because Walker would keep the interloper, Hannah Chase, away from Jake. Very likely there was an understanding between Jake and Leslie. Certainly there had been a warm familiarity between them. Still, Hannah thought with a touch of scorn, what did she care about any of these small-town concerns? They were nothing to her. And neither was Jake McCabe.

In spite of her quick brittle thoughts, she felt that the day had been marred in some obscure way by the meeting in the post office. It had been, up until then, one of the most exciting mornings she had experienced in a long time. She wanted somehow to bring that feeling back, to preserve it so she'd remember it just as it was.

She stayed up late that night, with Samson in his basket beside her, writing on her word processor. "A Day in the Life of a Country Vet," she called the piece. When she'd finished, she read it over and wondered what Bob Anderson would think of it.

CHAPTER FOUR

"BUT THEY LOOK BEAUTIFUL!" Hannah exclaimed, lifting the plastic covers from the dry cleaning she was picking up. "How did you ever...? I mean, you even mended the tear in the silk."

The little woman behind the counter gave her a mild look over her glasses. "Oh, I couldn't let that get by me—such a lovely material. I enjoyed doing it."

Hannah glanced at the bill—it would have been twice as much in the city, she knew—and reached into her handbag. "You haven't charged anything for the sewing," she said, handing over money. "Please, you must let me—"

The woman waved the words away as she made change. "Goodness, didn't cost anything but a few minutes of my time. I told you, I enjoyed doing it."

Going back out to her car and laying the clothes carefully across the seat, Hannah thought once again how life in Harrison Falls was something that took a bit of getting used to.

SHE WAS WEARING a simple dress of soft blue silk when Walker Harrison came to pick her up on Saturday afternoon. She had no idea what the occasion called for, but she suspected the Harrisons lived in a style quite different from that of Zelda Miles and the other townspeople she'd met. Plain but elegant would be a safe bet, she decided. Walker's reaction when she came to the door appeared to bear this out. His eyes widened slightly as he said, "Well! I don't think I fully appreciated Miss Hannah Chase when I met her last week in the post office. Perhaps we should do the introductions over again." He himself was dressed in white cord trousers and a yellow knit shirt, and again Hannah had the impression of expensive casualness.

She laughed and pulled the door shut behind her. "I'm still feeling my way here in Harrison Falls. I'm never sure what's right—the inhabitants always manage to surprise me somehow."

His eyes were still admiring her. "I'm sure you'd be just right even in a burlap bag."

"It hasn't come to that yet, thank goodness!"

They made their way down the steps to where Walker's sports car waited.

"You found a baby-sitter, I take it?" he asked, helping her in and closing the door for her. "Mrs. Miles?"

"Yes, Zelda kindly offered to help. Luckily the puppy's sleeping a little longer between feedings now."

"Wonderful. Then you can relax and enjoy the day. Unless you're planning on storing everything away in your head and writing about us later."

Hannah smiled as he walked around the car, got in and turned the key in the ignition. "You know, I might just do that?"

"Ha! Well, I'll certainly be on my best behavior."

Both of them laughed and then the car backed out of the driveway and roared powerfully up the quiet street.

Perfect, Hannah thought as they followed the long winding driveway up to the Harrison home. It was exactly the sort of place she'd pictured. First citizens of the town, founders and benefactors, old money—it had to look just like this. A handsome, pillared white house, manicured grounds, all set among rolling hills. Behind the house were roomy stables and a riding ring, with fenced acres of lush pasture surrounding everything. Today it was thronged with guests, and a tent for refreshments had been set up near the swimming pool. Apparel seemed to range from jodhpurs to graceful flowered tea dresses, and Hannah felt quite comfortable that she'd chosen right.

They were greeted by Leslie Harte—dressed for the country in a silk shirt, long divided skirt and boots, her blond hair tied back with a velvet ribbon. She stood before the entrance to the house with a distinguished-looking white-haired man.

"Miss Chase, welcome. May I call you Hannah? This is my father, Peyton Harrison. Father, Hannah is the newspaperwoman I told you about."

Peyton Harrison opened the passenger door and handed her out with old-world gallantry. "Welcome indeed, Miss Chase. I do hope you're enjoying your stay in Harrison Falls."

"Oh, I am, and it's most kind of you to have me here today."

"And this is my daughter, Bethany," Leslie said, motioning forward a girl who appeared to be about Carrie McCabe's age.

"Hello, Bethany," Hannah said, extending her hand.

The girl shook it indifferently and without meeting Hannah's eyes. "How do you do," she murmured perfunctorily, and then, to Leslie, "May I go now, Mother? I want to see if Major's ready."

"I'm sure Major's fine," Leslie said, "but all right, if you must." She shook her head helplessly as the girl, blond like her mother and wearing expensive boots, jodhpurs and knit shirt, hurried away without a farewell to any of them. A slightly petulant face, Hannah thought, a child too much indulged, perhaps. She couldn't help contrasting her with sturdy, freckled Carrie, whom she'd taken to at once.

"Quite a turnout," Walker remarked, gazing over the rows of cars parked in the taller grass beyond the driveway. Hannah saw a number of Mercedes, Jaguars and Cadillacs. Obviously the tri-county hunt club attracted the cream of society in these parts.

"Walker, take this young lady around and show her the grounds," Peyton Harrison ordered. "See that she has refreshments and introduce her to people."

"Yes, sir." Walker snapped a mock salute. "This way, Miss Chase. What will you see first?"

Leslie Harte interrupted with a laugh. "Skip the clowning, brother. Just be sure you have her back at the ring by the time the events start. Jake's coming a little later—we want to wait for him to start things. Do make yourself at home, Hannah."

"I should tell you," Hannah remarked as they turned to walk away, "that the whole idea of fox hunting turns me off."

Walker paused long enough to give her a surprised look and then to laugh good-naturedly. "Is *that* what you've been thinking?" he demanded. "Gosh, we don't chase real foxes."

"You don't?"

"No, we just drag scent across the trail and let the dogs take off. Good exercise for them and for us. Everyone has a day in the open and comes back feeling hungry."

"I admit to feeling relieved," Hannah said with a quick smile. "All right, lead on. Which way first?"

It was an hour of colorful impressions, introductions, of relaxed strolling over the meticulously cared-for grounds of the Harrison estate. Walker Harrison pointed out the barns and stables, introduced her to the head groom, showed her where the riding trails began. He guided her around the Olympic-size swimming pool where some of the younger guests were already splashing and shouting. After that, they went inside the house, and she looked admiringly at the spacious high-ceilinged rooms, their walls hung with paintings, their floors covered with Oriental rugs in lush reds and blues.

"It's beautiful," Hannah said. "Did your father build the house?"

"His father," Walker said. "Before that there were two other Harrisons here. I think the first one lived in a log cabin, and the second in a small farmhouse. In fact you can still see the cellar stones of that down in the south meadow."

"How nice to have such a long history in one place." She turned to smile up at him as he held open the front door for her and was startled to see how intently he was watching her, his eyes alive with interest and with something more personal, a look of unmistakable attraction.

"Well!" she said brightly. "When do those events start? Your sister said we mustn't miss them. Who's taking part, anyway?"

"Only the kids today. Things should be getting under way very shortly, I would guess," he said, resuming his role of amiable host. "The main attraction appears to have arrived."

Hannah glanced down toward the lower slope of the lawn where Leslie now stood by herself. Peyton Harrison had moved away to chat with his cronies, and the familiar Jeep Cherokee was just pulling up the drive.

Hannah felt an odd little jolt of her heart as Jake McCabe swung out in that loose, long-legged way she had come to know. Carrie was with him, hopping out on her side and at once extending her hand politely to Leslie Harte.

"Main attraction?" Hannah murmured.

"Oh, yes. Those two have been an item for some time."

"Really." Hannah watched with a curious sense of distance as Jake walked around and kissed Leslie lightly on the cheek. Kisses could be quite meaningless, of course—witness that one in the Rittenmyers' pasture last week. She'd felt herself held so tightly, and the touch of his lips on hers had seemed so intense, so...meaningful. Almost like the beginning of something—but of course it hadn't been that. Goodness, she'd made it abundantly clear to him that his kiss meant nothing to her.

"...like it better if his practice weren't quite so, er, folksy," Walker was saying.

"I'm sorry. What did you say?" She turned to face him.

"Just that I think Leslie would like it better if he was in a somewhat more...elevated situation professionally. That old house he practices out of, when he could just as well be in a new up-to-date clinic with all the very best equipment. That sort of thing really rattles Leslie."

"Oh? I did get the impression, though, that his house is very well fitted out with everything he needs."

"Yes, probably. I just think Les would like it better if he had somebody other than old Tully taking his phone messages, that sort of thing. A little more class, in other words."

Hannah glanced back at the little group at the end of the lawn. "Yes, of course," she murmured, under-

standing quite clearly how someone like Leslie Harrison
Harte would take a dim view of a client drinking coffee
in the kitchen or of puppies being kept underfoot in
cardboard boxes.

"Well!" Walker said brightly. "Let's join the festivi-
ties, shall we?"

They walked across the gently sloping lawn, which was
shaded by huge oaks and maples. From the other direction, out toward the stables, Bethany was hurrying toward her mother. Hannah heard her say, "Mother, for
heaven's sake, aren't we ready to start *yet?* Major's been
saddled for an hour, and he's getting fidgety."

"Yes, of course, darling," Leslie said soothingly.
"Come and say hello to Dr. McCabe and Carrie."

"Hi," the girl said, and looked away.

"We'll get things started any moment," Leslie promised. "Oh, look, here's Walker with Hannah. Hi, you
two, come on—we're ready to start the young people's
events."

Carrie ran to Hannah's side to greet her, and over her
head Hannah caught Jake's look. A slight dip of his
head in greeting, a glance from her to Walker and back
again, his expression slightly stiff, or so it seemed to her.
Then Walker stepped forward and he and Jake shook
hands, and the moment was bridged by Leslie's chatter.

"Beth, why don't you give Carrie a chance to ride
Major?" she said gaily. "I'm sure she'd enjoy that."

"Oh, for heaven's sake, Mother," Bethany snapped.
"You know how sensitive Major's mouth is! Passing
him around for strangers to ride would absolutely ruin
him. Carrie can ride Lady's Maid—she's good and
steady."

Hannah was, for a moment, full of fury on Carrie's
behalf, especially when she thought of the beautiful lit-

tle mare that would belong to the girl in another week. She should have had her own horse here, Hannah thought angrily. She saw Carrie bite her lower lip—not so much with hurt, she suspected, as with repressed anger. Then Carrie said calmly, "That would be okay, Bethany. I remember Lady's Maid. She'll do fine."

"Great," Jake said, and gave his daughter a smile. "Why don't you two girls go get ready? What's the first event, Leslie?"

"The barrel race. It's all set up, and after that the obstacle thing. We'll finish with the balloons."

The girls walked away, Bethany striding ahead, followed by Carrie, in blue jeans and a casual T-shirt. If Leslie was planning on marrying Jake and creating a combined family with the two girls as loving "sisters," she had a mountain-size job ahead of her, Hannah thought with sudden amusement. But the amusement turned to a bitter taste in her mouth as the notion grew on her. She turned to Walker and asked abruptly, "Where do we stand to watch all this?"

"This way—over by the ring," he said, and took her elbow. She could feel Jake's eyes on her as they walked away.

THERE WERE TWELVE young riders for the barrel race, which involved skirting a number of barrels that had been placed along a course. The event called for quick turns and skillful riding, and Bethany Harte easily led the group on her high-spirited black gelding, Major. Carrie gamely guided the stodgy Lady's Maid through the turns, but finished far behind. She was grinning, anyway, Hannah noticed, and she gave a good-natured wave in her father's direction as ribbons were handed out to everyone, winners and losers alike.

"It's not a real competition, of course," Leslie explained, but Hannah had seen the intensity of Bethany's expression as she'd flashed by and guessed that for her, at least, the rivalry was real.

"Now they'll set up the cavallettis for the obstacle course," Leslie went on, and Hannah, standing with Walker, Leslie and Jake on the sidelines, watched as three white-painted poles were set up some distance apart and at varying heights, with the highest only about twelve inches from the turf.

"Just some easy jumps, but it's good experience," Leslie said. Hannah watched as the young riders, eight for this event, took the obstacles in stride. Again, however, Bethany on Major went sailing over without even flicking a hoof against the poles. Polite applause greeted them, but it was Carrie McCabe who produced delighted laughter when plodding Lady's Maid stopped dead in front of the twelve-inch cavalletti and refused to budge. Quickly and gracefully Carrie slid out of the saddle, hopped over the pole herself and coaxed Lady's Maid to jump it with an empty saddle. Then she bowed to the crowd, patting the horse affectionately while the onlookers laughed spontaneously.

"A born clown," Hannah heard Jake say quietly and turned to see him shaking his head with a grin.

"And a born horsewoman, from what I can see," Hannah said.

Two spots of color had appeared in Leslie's cheeks. "Oh, we all think Carrie's a perfect darling," she said, immediately, reinforcing Hannah's vision of the happy household Leslie was trying to promote.

What happened a moment later, Hannah suspected, was seen by almost none of the onlookers, for it happened so quickly. At the edge of the ring close to where

Hannah was standing, the two girls, Bethany and Carrie, had dismounted and were waiting for the next event.

"Honestly, Carrie, can't you get that old nag to do any better than that?" Bethany snapped, and with a short whip hit the docile mare sharply across the rump. Lady's Maid whinnied and shied, but Carrie managed to calm her and the whole incident passed without heads even turning in their direction. Hannah had the distinct impression Bethany would have loved to inflict the blow on Carrie.

Moments later the balloon event was announced. "This one's just pure fun," Leslie told her. "See? It's done in partners. Six on that side of the ring and six over here. They ride toward each other carrying water-filled balloons, which they have to exchange in midfield. Father times them—quickest team wins."

Bethany and Carrie were paired; Hannah was sure it was under instructions from Leslie. After five sets of young riders had floundered across the ring and managed to exchange balloons or else fumble and drop them to break wetly in the dust, Bethany kicked her heels into Major's sides and went trotting out to the center, with Carrie coming toward her from the other side on Lady's Maid. At the halfway point, with neither horse stopping, the two girls held out their balloons. They reached, fumbled, leaned toward each other, and then a sudden explosion of water cascaded over Bethany, drenching her shirt, her spotless jodhpurs, dripping down onto her boots. Carrie and Lady's Maid trotted calmly across to the other side with their balloon intact.

The crowd, which had held its breath for a second, burst into laughter and applause, and Walker called out, "Should have worn a swimsuit for that one, Beth!"

Hannah could feel Leslie go rigid beside her, then heard her tight, uncomfortable laugh. "Well, fortunately swimming's on the program, anyway," she said, and took Jake's arm in a possessive gesture. "And now that all that's over, I'm starved. Come on, everyone, let's head for the refreshments."

Walker's attentive hand was under Hannah's elbow at once, guiding her away, and Hannah had only a moment to glance in Carrie's direction as she dismounted and started to lead her horse toward the stables. The girl lifted her head and looked across the ring, catching Hannah's eye for a fraction of a second. Her small secret grin was an unmistakable communication between them. Hannah smiled back and gave her a quick wink.

She spent the rest of the afternoon listening, absorbing, watching, as the party eddied and flowed around her. Walker was the most gallant of hosts, leaving her only at her insistence when she could see that other guests were seeking him out. For the most part he stayed close to her, and Hannah felt comfortable in his easygoing presence. She met dozens of new people, tried to remember all their names but found it impossible; she enjoyed the food, the champagne—recommended by Peyton Harrison himself—and the general atmosphere of good living and luxury that the Harrison estate exuded. Bethany reappeared after a brief absence, freshly dressed in an outfit exactly like the one that had been drenched. Hannah guessed her closet contained rows of such clothing. Leslie's daughter and Carrie didn't seek each other out. Bethany spent most of her time with a small group of similarly dressed girls. But Hannah could see that Carrie was mingling easily in the crowd, talking to other young people, but also to the adults—even bending close to an old lady who was obviously hard of hearing and shouting, "I'll save a jar of it for you, Mrs. Prindle. It's wonderful on toast!"

More than once Hannah looked for Jake, but invariably he was being monopolized by Leslie, who seemed to refuse to let him out of her sight or grasp. Only toward evening when some of the guests changed for swimming did she see him alone. By chance both Leslie and Walker had been called to the front of the house to see off some departing guests. Hannah watched from the edge of the pool as Jake, sun-browned and lithe, long legs gleaming wet in the late rays of the sun, climbed to the diving board, poised there and then jackknifed cleanly into the water. She watched as he swam with strong strokes across the pool and back. Then he made for the edge of the pool and swung himself up without using the ladder, reached for a towel on the table and turned to see Hannah standing there.

She saw the surprise in his face.

"Well! Enjoying yourself?" he asked as he rubbed vigorously.

"Very much. It's a wonderful spot here. And the Harrisons do seem to know how to throw a good party."

"Did you see the stable? It's really quite a place."

"Walker showed it to me from the outside."

"Wait till I throw some clothes on—I'll take you over there."

"Fine."

Hannah kept her voice level and purposely did not betray the sudden excitement she felt, but as he ducked into the poolside cabana to change she stole a look toward the driveway and the front lawn to see if Walker and Leslie were headed toward them yet. They were both still involved in conversation with a group of guests. Jake was back in seconds, however, his hair uncombed and still curling damply from his swim, and they started off in the direction of the big red-painted stable with its immaculate white trim.

"Carrie seems to be enjoying herself," Hannah commented, nodding toward a group of teenagers who were playing badminton with more hilarity than accuracy.

"She is, but do you know how hard I had to argue with her to come? She felt she was neglecting her bees."

"I wish she could have been here with her own horse."

"It'll be all the better for the wait," he said.

It was ordinary talk, but somehow less intimate, less personal than conversations they'd had before. Something lay between them, Hannah sensed—some obstacle that had not been there the other times they'd been together. Leslie's possessiveness and Walker Harrison's obvious interest in Hannah were outside elements that had intruded. But that was ridiculous, she told herself quickly. Nothing had started between them, nor did she want it to. Staying away from romantic entanglements had been her rule up to now; no reason to change that. Besides, he and Leslie were obviously an established pair.

Even so, as they walked along together through lengthening shadows, she could feel currents of almost physical vibration between them. She tried to match her stride to his longer one, and when they reached the stable door and he let her pass through first, her arm brushed his lightly, sending tiny shock waves through her.

"Well!" she said, bridging the moment hastily. "This is a showplace, too, I see."

"Oh, the Harrisons never do anything halfway," he said, smiling down at her, and Hannah could not help thinking, *How right you are.*

The stable was fascinating. Twenty stalls ranged along one side, faced with twenty more opposite, separated by a wide aisle. The floor was concrete, and there were hoses and drains for shampooing the horses. Each stall had its own window and fan, and a brass nameplate on the stall door. At the end of each row was an outsized stall.

"For foaling," Jake explained when they came to these. "And over here's the tack room."

Hannah saw rows of saddles and bridles and on the wall pictures of horses and their riders, most of them Harrisons, along with a vast array of ribbons won in competitions. A smaller room adjoined it and Hannah could see a cot and a leather chair. She glanced at Jake.

"Head groom usually stays there at foaling time," he said.

"Nicer than a good many houses I've seen," she commented. Only a few of the stalls were occupied now, with horses quietly swishing their tails and stamping. Hannah had seen others out in the rail-fenced pasture. Jake stopped at one of the stalls and gave the horse in it a quick scrutiny.

"One of my patients," he said. When she came closer to look, he added, "Lame leg. We've been keeping him quiet."

Hannah nodded, but she was more aware of the man's nearness than the matter of the horse. Standing next to him in the dim shadowy stable with its sweet smell of hay, she could feel her knees going weak in an oddly uncontrollable way. *I'm not seventeen,* she insisted to herself. *I'm twenty-seven. What's the matter with me?*

Then, without warning, his arm slid around her shoulder and she turned her face up to him. He bent his head and kissed her, a long, soft, lingering kiss. Hannah leaned toward him, her body pressing along the length of his as his other arm came around her, holding her close.

Footsteps outside made them pull apart, although they sought one another's eyes and held the gaze for a long moment, as if each was seeking something in the other. Then Leslie Harte was standing in the doorway.

"Goodness, I couldn't think what had happened to you two!" she said, looking from one to the other, but Hannah, turning away from Jake hastily, sensed the sharp edge of anger in her voice.

"Jake was just showing me the stables," she said, trying to subdue her emotions and sound rational, but conscious all the time of the pounding of her heart—so loud that she thought Leslie must surely hear it, too. "They're really beautiful."

"Oh, good. I'm glad you're getting to see everything." Habit and poise were coming to Leslie's rescue, holding her together, but Hannah was sure there was fury smoldering underneath. "Jake, would you be a dear and come talk to Jeff Crewes about his yellow Lab? He's asking me all sorts of questions I can't answer. I believe he's thinking of taking her on the show circuit."

"Sure. Where is he?" Jake moved reluctantly away from Hannah just as Peyton Harrison appeared behind his daughter. A pair of black-and-white border collies scampered at his heels.

"There she is!" he exclaimed at the sight of Hannah. "I've been looking for this lady."

"If you're planning on giving her the grand tour, it seems Jake beat you to it, Dad," Leslie said lightly, but again with the knife edge in her voice.

"Well, I'm sure he didn't show her Prince Hal. He's the one who started this whole thing," he explained to

Hannah, and as Leslie took Jake's arm possessively and led him off, Peyton Harrison escorted Hannah through the big double doors at the rear of the stable.

"Spends most of his time out in this special enclosure," Peyton Harrison was saying, "although some days he still wants to get out and run with the younger ones. We've lost track of how many colts he's sired, on our place and some of the other horse farms in this part of the state. There—isn't he a beauty?"

Hannah followed his pointing finger to a fenced-in area where a big chestnut stallion with a broad chest and flowing mane stood regally, switching his tail and tossing his head from time to time.

"Oh, he is!" Hannah said.

"Come on, Hal, come on, boy," Peyton Harrison called, and the horse turned his head alertly and came trotting over to them. Hannah murmured her admiration and patted the velvet nose that was thrust over the rail fence, but inside her, emotions were rolling and tumbling wildly. How had all this happened? Always in the past she had been able to maintain distance and aloofness. What was going wrong now?

Dusk was moving in softly, blue shadows and a dark golden sunset, by the time she parted from Peyton Harrison. By then she'd been introduced to most of the horses by name, had strolled with him over the grounds and even into the meadow to look at the foundation stones of the old farmhouse Walker had mentioned to her. "They don't build them like that anymore," Peyton had insisted. "Just see how those stones are joined...." At last they'd returned to the front lawn, where several departing guests claimed him. He excused himself, and Hannah, thinking about leaving and looking around for Walker, suddenly spotted him heading toward the stable with Jake beside him. They were talking together, and Jake, slightly taller, was bending his head toward Walker. Hannah frowned. She was beginning to feel weary and emotionally spent and wanted to ask Walker to drive her home, but she would have preferred not to encounter Jake again. Still, there seemed no way to accomplish that, so she strolled after them slowly.

She saw the two disappear inside the stable. She went on walking, reached the open door and paused there for a moment. Before she could pluck up her courage to go inside, she heard voices, Walker's and Jake's, and now the tone was not conversational and friendly, but decidedly antagonistic.

She heard Walker say, "But I don't see why not! It's just treatment." His voice had a sharp argumentative sound.

"It is not treatment. The horse is chronically lame," Jake retorted.

Walker muttered something she couldn't make out, and then Jake's voice rose angrily. "I know what you want, Walker, and you can forget it. You've got a prospective buyer for this horse, that's what it is. Well, I'm not going to help you dupe some poor unsuspecting soul by administering a painkiller to mask what's wrong with him."

Hannah heard strong decisive footsteps then, and Jake came stalking out of the stable, looking neither right nor left, his face set in a mask of fury.

"Jake, what's wrong?" she called out, and he gave her a surprised look.

"Why don't you ask your date?" he snapped, and strode away from her without stopping.

Walker followed him out a moment later, his face dark with anger, but seeing Hannah he seemed to transform it by an effort of will into its usual expression of relaxed good humor.

"I hope you were looking for me," he said with a grin.

"I was, as a matter of fact," she said, stumbling a little over the words and feeling uncomfortable. "I think it's high time I got home—Zelda will be worn out with puppy-sitting."

"I'd stop you if I could," he said, taking her elbow and guiding her back along the track toward the house. "But if your mind's made up..."

"I really think I should," she said. "It's been a perfectly wonderful day. I can't think when I've had such a good time." *Ask your date.* Jake had fairly flung the words at her a moment ago, but now she found it impossible to bring the matter up with Walker. Besides, it was quite possible she had misinterpreted what she'd heard. These were country concerns, about which she knew less than nothing. The two men were obviously friends. Hannah glanced at the man walking beside her. Or were they? She gave herself an inward shake. She was making too much of it, jumping to conclusions on incomplete evidence. Something a good newspaperwoman would never do, she reminded herself sternly.

CHAPTER FIVE

HANNAH, SITTING ON Zelda's porch steps in the spring sunshine a week later, watched as Sam struggled in his basket, trying to find his feet to bring himself upright. Birds were loud in the trees around her, and from the back where Zelda kept a few chickens came busy clucking sounds. Laughing at the puppy's exertions, Hannah hadn't noticed anyone approaching until a shadow fell across her. Looking up, she let out a small scream.

An apparition completely covered in white, faceless under a concealing hood, stood at the foot of the steps. If it had been dusky twilight instead of midmorning, Hannah thought her heart would have stopped altogether.

"Hi, Hannah, it's me," said a small voice, and the apparition moved, unzipping the hood. "I didn't mean to scare you. I just wanted to show you my new bee outfit."

Hannah gave a shaky laugh. "Carrie! Goodness, you did give me a start. Well, it's quite something, I must say. And happy birthday, by the way. Today's the day, isn't it?"

"Yes, it is, and my father's going to kill me." The girl fumbled to push back the bee veil.

Hannah grinned. "Oh, I doubt that. Not on your birthday, surely."

"Well, he will, sort of. The UPS man just stopped at the house and I saw the package was from the beekeepers' supply company, so I opened it. Well, see, I figured it was something for me, but I didn't figure on it being a surprise—you know what I mean...."

"And besides, you were too excited to wait."

"I guess that was part of it," Carrie admitted sheepishly. "But now he's going to be good and mad, because I'm sure it was supposed to be my birthday present. And he must have wanted to give it to me at the party."

Hannah thought of the dainty mare with the creamy mane and tail but said nothing to contradict the girl.

"Your dad's not home now?"

"No, he's out on calls."

"You could put it back in the package."

"That wouldn't be honest, really."

"Well, no." Hannah felt vaguely embarrassed for having suggested it. "I'm afraid you'll just have to take your lumps."

Carrie nodded. "Hey, you didn't forget about the party, did you?"

"Goodness, no. I'll be there."

"Good. Look, I brought something to show you," the girl went on, sounding a little shy. She held out a manila folder. Hannah took it and peeked inside. It seemed to be a sheaf of sketches.

"Carrie! Did you do these?"

"Yes, well, I do that sometimes. You can look at them while I take this stuff out to Zelda's chickens."

Hannah glanced at what she held in her other hand. Parts of a hive, she thought. "What on earth is that?"

"Oh, wax moths got into one of my hives and ruined the comb—see?" She held it up and Hannah could see the webbing and tunneling of the destructive pests. "I'll take it out to the chickens," Carrie explained. "They love wax moths. They'll clean the whole thing up in no time so I can use it again."

"Goodness." Hannah shook her head in wonderment. "How much you beekeepers have to know."

"Oh, you just learn one step at a time," Carrie said modestly. "Like driving in traffic, my dad says."

She strode off in the direction of the chicken coop and Hannah turned her attention again to the folder in her lap. The sketches, a half dozen of them, surprised her by their vigor. Not professional, not perfect, but full of life and motion, and all of horses and riders. Hannah could even recognize them—spirited Major taking the jumps easily, placid Lady's Maid clumping along with her head down. Carrie had captured the riders, too. She'd sketched Bethany accurately—straight back and trim posture. Her own image she had drawn with flying hair and loose shirttails, both feet sticking out awkwardly as she tried to urge Lady's Maid on.

"Carrie, these are wonderful!" she exclaimed when the girl returned. Carrie blushed and looked at the ground. Hannah hesitated for a moment and then said suddenly, "May I keep them just for this afternoon? To show Zelda? I'll bring them back when we come to the party."

"Okay—well, sure."

"Good." Hannah watched the girl make her way along the path and disappear into the shrubbery. Then she picked up basket and folder and went inside. She found Zelda, aproned and flushed, mixing cake batter in the big kitchen.

"Is that for Carrie's party?" Hannah asked, putting down the puppy's basket and sitting at the kitchen table.

"Yes. Seven layers with boiled icing. What's that folder?"

"She was just here." Hannah told Zelda about the bee suit and the sketches. "And I've had an idea." She described it to Zelda, who never missed a beat of her wooden spoon while she listened and nodded.

"Wonderful. Great idea. But will you do an errand for me first? I need chicken feed. You remember where the feed store is. Take the truck—you'll be back in no time."

"All right."

Swinging into the driver's seat of the rusty old pickup, Hannah could not resist an inward smile at the picture of herself, in jeans and denim shirt, coaxing the old machine into life and bumping down the dirt driveway to the county road. Could this possibly be a New York City career woman whose only previous contact with the country had been the manicured lawns of her grandfather's Long Island home? During the past week she'd had ample opportunity to learn that life in the country was anything but the quiet contemplative existence she had thought it. Mostly, she admitted with a faint pang of regret, she had kept herself busy, with her writing and with chores for Zelda, in order to avoid Jake McCabe. And if she could have thought of a logical way to dodge the party at his house tonight she would have done so. The thing she had dreaded all her life—an entanglement—had suddenly loomed as more of a problem here in Harrison Falls than in the fast-paced life she'd left behind. Each time she was with him she felt the pull of attraction between them, yet his angry outburst outside the Harrison stables the week before had confused and unsettled her, and now she was more than ever determined to keep her distance. Emotional involvements were something she could do without, Hannah reminded herself. Her career had become important to her because it was the one dependable thing in her life, the one constant reliable element she could cling to. She had no intention of changing that emphasis now.

As if sensing her need, Zelda had filled the week with chores, errands, activities. "Why can't you? Anybody who can drive a car can drive a truck," she had said matter-of-factly, and Hannah had tried it, cautiously at first but gaining courage as the old machine sputtered and balked but finally responded to her coaxing. Now she felt quite at home driving toward McCluskey's feed store. She'd been there before with Zelda, and she veered into the parking lot and around to the loading platform with all the familiarity of a native.

"Good morning, Mr. McCluskey," she said, walking into the high-ceilinged warehouse that smelled of grain and malt and fresh hay. "Zelda wants fifty pounds of chicken feed."

"Be right with you, Miss Chase. Soon's as I load up this last order."

"Take your time," Hannah said, and strolled away from him, reading labels for goat pellets and sweet-feed and stopping to stroke an enormous tabby sleeping on a pile of burlap bags.

"Hi there."

The voice behind her made her whirl around. Jake had just come in. The sun at his back in the doorway framed his square shoulders. Hannah put a hand over her eyes and peered up into his face, but it was shadowed. He took three steps toward her, and inside, out of the glare, she could see him better. His blue eyes were gazing down at her with an intense, studying look.

"We haven't seen much of you this week," he said, resting his weight on one leg and hooking his thumbs in the belt loops of his jeans.

"Oh—I've been—that is, Zelda's been keeping me quite busy. Her church had a social, and we had to plow up a new section of garden for the late things—Zelda believes in staggering her planting. Also she taught me to bake bread one day. *And* she's got me driving the truck."

"Sounds as if it doesn't leave much time for writing." His tone was formal, polite.

"Not a lot, but I manage." His nearness was disquieting. Hannah felt his presence like a tangible warmth, something that communicated itself to her in waves, causing small tremors and uncertainties deep inside her.

"How's Sam?"

"Oh, coming along famously. He's gaining weight and trying to stand up. Mostly he falls down flat with all four legs splayed out, but one of these days he'll make it."

"And here you are at McCluskey's, the social center of Harrison Falls." He smiled for the first time, and some of the stiffness between them seemed to dissolve.

"Yes, for fifty pounds of chicken feed. Zelda's busy with the birthday cake."

"And I'm here for fifty pounds of dog kibble. Can I load yours on the truck for you?"

"Oh, I'm sure Mr. McCluskey—"

"Just to show you chivalry isn't dead." He grinned and before she could protest, swung a heavy bag of chicken feed onto his shoulder, walking with his long easy stride through the warehouse and out to the loading platform.

"I've got Miss Chase's order, Bob," he called out to the owner.

"Right you are, Doc."

Hannah stopped long enough to pick up the slip McCluskey scribbled for her, then followed Jake outside. The bag was in the truck and he was standing on the platform in the relaxed posture she had seen before, arms folded in front of him.

"There was something on the radio this morning about rain, but I'm not convinced," he said, scanning the sky where a few small cottony clouds drifted against the blue.

She paused awkwardly beside him, feeling once again the small hidden stirrings of attraction. She was thankful they were outdoors here on the platform instead of inside, in the dim dusty warehouse with only the purring of the feed-store cat as a background. Somehow she always felt vulnerable when she was alone with him, and out of control, something she had always disliked. She needed to see herself as independent, in charge of her own destiny.

"I hope it stays nice for the party," she said in a small voice.

"I'm glad you're coming." He looked down at her suddenly, and then surprised her by putting out his hand to touch her arm. A shiver went shooting through her like quicksilver.

"Oh, I wouldn't miss it. Well, I'd better get going. Zelda's waiting for me," she said lamely. She whirled around and hurried down the platform steps, swinging up into the truck and starting it, wheeling out toward the road with only a wave of her hand from the open window.

"Well! That was quick," Zelda said when she returned. The cake was in the oven and already smelled delectable.

"Yes. I saw Jake there. He loaded the feed onto the truck for me." Hannah was standing in the middle of the kitchen with both hands pressed together.

"Any trouble?" Zelda asked, glancing at her curiously.

"Trouble? What sort of trouble?"

"With the ignition on the truck," Zelda said dryly.

"Oh, no. No, everything was fine." Hannah turned and hurried out of the kitchen and upstairs.

For the rest of the day she stayed in her room with the door shut, hunched over her worktable with the word processor shoved to one side as she toiled with pen and paper, taking care to write simply and to leave plenty of margin and space between lines. She doubted that it had ever taken her so long to write so few words. Once Zelda tiptoed in, glancing over her shoulder and leaving her a glass of milk and a sandwich, then tiptoeing out just as quietly. At four-thirty she returned, poking her head in and announcing the time. "Have to start thinking about getting over there," she said.

"It's okay. Come on in, Zelda. I'm just finishing my clean copy. Here. You can look it over while I grab a quick bath."

She returned moments later in terry-cloth robe and damp towel to ask eagerly, "Is it all right, do you think?"

Zelda shook her head wonderingly. "Oh, it's just perfect. She'll be thrilled. You are quite a lady, Miss

Hannah Chase. Come on now, let's get a move on. I've got the food all packed up.''

Hannah, who was beginning to have an instinctive understanding of social matters in Harrison Falls, felt that a high-fashion statement would not be called for today as it had been for the party on the Harrison estate. So she slipped into her denim skirt and a fresh pink shirt, thrust her feet into low sandals and brushed her hair back loosely, letting it fall to her shoulders. Then she went hurrying down the steps to help Zelda pack the casserole dishes into baskets.

"We'll come back for the cake later," Zelda said. "Here, you carry this one. And what about Sam? He'd better come, don't you think?"

"Oh, I do. I can manage his basket.''

"Okay, fine. Are we ready?''

Loaded with their burdens, they made their way slowly along the path to the house next door. As they approached, a thought struck Hannah with such force that she stopped still in the middle of the path and turned to Zelda.

"Will Leslie Harte—do you think she'll be here tonight?'' she asked.

"I didn't have a look at the guest list," Zelda said in her dry, teasing way. "But my guess is no.''

"You don't think so? But I thought she and Jake were sort of... you know, involved.''

Zelda shrugged in an offhand manner. "Who knows? I just don't think backyard barbecues are Leslie's style. Come on, let's get going.''

Zelda was proven right. The "guest list" was not long. In addition to Hannah and Zelda, it consisted of Tully and his two grandchildren, twins who were friends of Carrie's. They were a boy and a girl—both towheaded and sunburned—in her class at school, as they explained to Hannah. While Jake took charge of the grill outside, first pouring soft drinks and lemonade for everyone, and while Hannah and Zelda set the table on the wide veranda and placed Zelda's potato salad, pickled beets and squash casserole on it, the three young people took Sam onto the lawn. They let him struggle and roll in the soft grass as he tried to walk, flopping down each time. Zack, Jake's golden retriever, observed the scene with curious ears forward, but offered no objection and even made friendly overtures by licking the puppy.

"Two or three more weeks, he'll have you all chasing him," Tully called out from the porch step where he sat with his pipe. "Hannah, you've done wonders for that little runt," he said over his shoulder.

"She's a wonder-working lady," Jake said, coming up the steps with a trayful of hot dogs and hamburgers in their toasted rolls. "Come on, everybody! Let's get this party under way."

Hannah glanced at him and their eyes locked for a moment. Then she looked quickly away and went to return the puppy to his basket.

"Presents next or birthday cake?" Jake asked, when they had demolished the hot dogs and hamburgers, scraped the salad bowl clean and left the whole table looking as if it had been fallen upon by hungry invading hordes.

"Foolish question," Zelda chided. "Presents, of course. How long do you expect this child to wait?"

Twelve-year-old Hank was obviously disappointed, but his sister, Ellen, applauded excitedly, and Carrie's eyes lit up.

"Well, the bee outfit, of course, has been opened already," Jake said with a meaningful look at his daughter.

"I said I was sorry, Dad." But Carrie's eyes were twinkling happily as she got up, hurried around to him and gave him a hug. "It's just beautiful."

"Well, here's something to go with it then," Zelda said, and produced a bulky package from under the table. Carrie opened it carefully and brought out an oddly shaped metal device that Hannah frowned at and tried to identify. One-half of it looked like a hat for the Tin Man in *The Wizard of Oz,* the other half like a miniature accordion.

"A new smoker!" Carrie shouted. "Zelda, it's wonderful. So much better than my old one." Seeing Hannah's bewildered look, she explained. "Sometimes you have to smoke the bees a little, see. Just to get them out of the way when you're working. You make a fire in this part—" she pointed to the hat shape "—and then you squeeze the bellows part."

Hannah shook her head in wonderment. "Goodness," she murmured.

"Here, Carrie. This is from Hank and me," Ellen said, handing her a limp package wrapped in tissue paper. The T-shirt Carrie pulled out had large colorful letters across the front—NIAGARA FALLS. "It's from our trip last year."

"And this is from me," Tully said. "They ought to go real good together." The red-and-blue baseball cap read Harrison Falls Tigers. Carrie squealed with delight and put it on at once. "Oh, I love them both! I love everything!"

A little shyly, Hannah passed over the manila folder Carrie had left with her earlier. "This is from me, Carrie."

Carrie looked curiously at her and at the folder before opening it. Then she took out the small sheaf of papers, now bound together with clips and bearing a title page: "The Magic Pony."

"What *is* it?" she breathed.

"It's your drawings. I wrote a story to go with them."

Carrie's face was a picture of wonder and delight, but it was Jake's expression that caused Hannah's heart to jump. His eyes were fixed on her in a look of sudden surprise and something else she couldn't read. He was moved, she thought. Touched that she'd done this for his daughter. Well, that was a natural response. Carrie meant the world to him, of course. There was no more to it than that.

"Once upon a time," Carrie began reading, and everyone around the table listened with rapt attention as she read the brief story aloud—the story of a pony unable to jump the lowest fence and laughed at by the crowd. But one girl believed in the pony and encouraged her, and at the crucial moment the plodding pony magically lifted her head and hooves and went sailing over the jumps like a champion.

"Oh, Hannah, it's a beautiful story!" Carrie cried. "It ought to be in a real book. Not my drawings, your story."

"I don't think either one of us is experienced enough for a real book." Hannah laughed. "But this is meant to encourage us. You practice your drawings and I'll work on story ideas, and one day we'll do a real one."

"Honestly?" Carrie was astonished.

"Why not?"

"Oh, what a great birthday!" Carrie exploded, and Zelda said, "Well, there's more to come. What about that cake?"

"I'll get it, Zelda," Hannah said quickly, feeling suddenly a little too full of emotion to sit quietly at the table.

"Why don't I come and help?" Jake suggested as Hannah pushed her chair back, and Zelda added, "Good. You two do that and the rest of us will clear away the wreckage. Somebody'd better look after the puppy, too."

"I'll do it," Hank volunteered, and as Hannah and Jake walked away, they could hear the clinking and scraping of dishes, along with laughter and voices.

"Your story was a tremendous hit," he said, holding the shrubbery aside for her to pass through.

"I had fun doing it. I'm glad she was pleased. And I meant it, you know, what I said. She has a lot of talent. Who knows, maybe one day she'll do something with it."

"Not many people would have been so thoughtful, though."

Hannah, feeling warm and self-conscious all the way down to her toes, changed the subject. "What about Foxfire? I thought you'd have brought her out by now. Is she in the shed?"

"Oh, she's there all right. But can you imagine Carrie sitting still for the party if she'd seen the horse first? Once the cake and ice cream are finished I'll send her out there. The bee outfit was a kind of red herring."

Hannah looked up at him, shaking her head. "I think you're enjoying it all as much as Carrie."

They had come to the end of the path and reached the back porch of Zelda's house. He opened the squeaky screen door and they stepped into the fragrant kitchen with its leftover baking smells.

"Thank you, Hannah. You helped make the day," he whispered.

"It wasn't anything. I didn't—" she began, but he tipped her chin up with one finger and kissed her softly. In the early evening stillness Hannah became aware of the smallest sounds—the clock ticking on Zelda's shelf, the movement of a branch against the window, her own heartbeat. He kissed her again, a deeper, more insistent kiss this time, and Hannah, not meaning to, not wanting to, put both arms up to encircle his neck and returned his kiss with a passion of her own. For a long time they held each other, until, with a little gasp, Hannah pushed away and laughed shakily. "Goodness, they'll be sending out a search party. We'd better get this cake over there."

He touched her hair lightly and said, "You're full of surprises, you know that? Just when I think I have you figured out, you turn around and do the unexpected."

"Then you'd better stop trying to figure me out," she said teasingly, moving away from him toward the table where the covered cake plate stood.

It was still light, with the long lingering sunset of a late spring evening, when they lit the candles. By the time the cake and ice cream were finished and all of them were sitting back luxuriously on the McCabes' wide veranda, there were only a few faint blue shadows creeping across the lawn.

"This was the best birthday ever," Carrie said emphatically. She was cradling Sam in her lap and wearing her Harrison Falls Tigers cap.

"Go on. You said the same thing last year," Zelda said with a wide grin.

"Well, it gets better every year. Zelda, the cake was scrumptious."

"Do you think you could stir yourself to go out to the shed for me?" Jake asked casually.

"Sure, Dad. What do you need?" Carrie pulled herself out of her chair and handed the puppy to Ellen.

"A package that came today—you'll see it as you go in. I left it there until I had a chance to get to it."

"Okay. Be right back."

Hannah found herself holding her breath as she watched the girl leave the porch and go around to the back. She waited, her glance seeking out Jake's face, and felt her tension mount as she waited for the cry of joy, the surprised shout. There was only silence. The shed door had creaked open, but not a sound came out.

"Jake, you and Hannah go see," Zelda whispered.

Tiptoeing, the two of them walked around the house and back to the big barnlike shed at the rear of the property. The door stood open and the last long rays of sunlight fell across the dusty floor. Carrie was standing inside the stall with Foxfire, arms around the horse's neck. The little mare wore a pink birthday ribbon on her halter, and was accepting the attention calmly. The girl's face was streaked with tears.

Jake's arm came around Hannah, and Hannah felt tears springing to her own eyes.

SHE SPOTTED the brown envelope on the table in Zelda's front hall when they returned home. She picked it up and saw that it was from Bob Anderson at the newspaper.

"Oh, Hannah, I'm sorry. In all the rush I forgot to tell you about that—it came this afternoon."

"That's okay. I'm headed for bed. How about you?"

"Soon as I put out the lights. See you tomorrow."

Carrying Sam's basket and the envelope, Hannah went upstairs. Once in her room, however, she didn't open her mail right away. Instead, she tossed it onto the bed, put the puppy's basket on the floor in its usual nighttime spot and went to throw open a window. Cool night breezes flooded in, and Hannah sank into a low chair near the window and felt the moist refreshing air against her face and body. She was feeling, in spite of the laughter and warmth of the birthday party, curiously downhearted—by something she couldn't immediately put her finger on. Then, out of the past, a memory came back to her. One special summer at her grandfather's house on Long Island. How old had she been? Nine, perhaps. And there had been, that year, a cook-and-butler couple, Millie and Edwin. Comfortably middle-aged and kind, they'd understood her loneliness from the beginning. They'd encouraged her to keep them company in the kitchen; Millie had let her help with cooking. Hannah had never been so happy, never felt so much a part of anyone's household. Then her mother had arrived for a weekend, had come upon her, aproned and floury, helping Millie make doughnuts, and had snatched her away angrily, back to the city, where she'd been obliged to finish out the hot and lonely summer in the company of a thin, severe nanny.

The most joyous time in her life taken away from her without a chance to make even a murmur of protest. Hannah had never quite forgotten the pain.

Something of that same warm feeling of belonging had been creeping over her day by day ever since she'd arrived in Harrison Falls. From that first bee sting and Jake's lively blue eyes looking down at her as he'd held the ice cube against her face, to the soft sensual kiss tonight in Zelda's kitchen, she had felt an increasing sense of rightness about it all. But what did Jake McCabe really feel about her? From all she could observe, he was firmly committed to Leslie Harte. Their attachment was of long-standing, and she, Hannah, was an outsider. And what about her own rule of no involvement? If she didn't become involved, she wouldn't be hurt, right? But how could she help it, when everything around her conspired daily to pull her further into the life here? Even though Jake might be the biggest part of it, it wasn't only Jake. There was Zelda and her quick understanding glance. Carrie and her bees. There was Mr. McCluskey at the feed store, the little woman at the dry cleaner's—all of them creeping into her life. But her thoughts kept returning to Jake as she remembered the feeling of his lips on hers, the way his arm stole around her as they'd stood together in the shed doorway. Wasn't it all going to prove just a repetition of that long-ago summer when joy and warmth had been snatched away from her and she'd been helpless to prevent it? And if so, wasn't the best plan to thwart her growing involvement with the town before that could happen?

Making a sudden decision, she got up and tiptoed out of the room, down the dim stairs where Zelda kept a tiny nightlight on, all the way to the front hall and the telephone. Before she could think further about it, she dialed.

"Bob? It's Hannah."

"Hannah, for Pete's sake, is something wrong?"

"Bob, it's only ten o'clock! That's not crisis time. I just wanted to talk to you."

"Oh. Did you get the envelope I sent?"

"It just came today. Haven't even opened it."

"Well, open it. You'll be amazed at how—"

"Wait a minute. I want to ask you something."

"Shoot."

"Can I come back to New York? When's that trial, anyway?"

"What's the matter? Getting cabin fever out there in the boondocks?"

Hannah swallowed hard. "Something like that."

"Well, I was going to get in touch with you. There's been a postponement. You'll have to stick it out a little longer."

Hannah felt her heart drop. "Oh, Bob, no. Really?"

"Hey, it can't be that bad. And keep those small-town stories coming. They're good, Hannah. Go open that envelope now. We'll be in touch."

Hannah put the telephone down slowly and climbed the stairs to her room. Once inside, she leaned wearily against the door for a moment, then walked to the bed and picked up the bulky envelope. When she opened it and tipped it up, a stream of smaller envelopes poured out. Letters? Hannah thought wonderingly. She opened one, then a second and a third, scanning them hastily. All letters, directed to her or to "the editor," all enthusiastic comments on her series of small-town articles. "Reminded me of things I'd forgotten..." "Loved the one about the country vet's round of calls..."

Now just take it easy, Hannah Chase, she told herself sternly, walking back to the open window. Put on the brakes. And before you let yourself go all soft and mushy over this small-town experience, remember who you are and what you do for a living. This cosy country life is not for you—never has been. Don't let yourself be fooled into thinking you can be something you're not. Sooner or later you're going to leave it all behind—lose the whole thing. So there's no use setting yourself up for heartbreak.

Hannah felt the cool breeze of evening against her flushed face. *Who am I kidding?* she asked herself wearily. *The only thing I'm worried about losing is Jake McCabe.*

CHAPTER SIX

WHEN SHE CAME down to breakfast a few days later, Hannah slipped a check under the sugar bowl that stood on Zelda's kitchen table. Zelda, coffeepot in one hand and a plateful of buttered toast in the other, eyed it critically.

"I swear it feels all wrong to take that, Hannah."

"Don't be silly." Hannah put the puppy basket down and slid into a chair at the table. "I'm eating like a longshoreman here, for one thing. That alone could send you into bankruptcy."

"Oh, pooh." Zelda set the plate down and poured coffee for both of them. "I love having somebody around the house—somebody to sit down at the table with. And as far as that room of yours goes, it was just sitting there empty."

"That may be, but I think it's a bargain, and you certainly deserve some return, considering all you've done for me."

"Go on." Zelda waved Hannah's words away and took a seat opposite her. She was wearing her usual jeans and today an oversize shirt that Hannah suspected might have belonged to the late Mr. Miles. "You've been here, how long? Three, four weeks? And I've come to think of you as a friend. I just feel it's all wrong to take money when I've gotten so much out of this myself."

Hannah felt the welling of emotion that seemed to visit her so often these days over simple things. Simple goodness, simple pleasures. "Well, I think I'm the one who's had all the benefit. And Sam, too, of course." She smiled down at the puppy, who was moving restlessly in his basket.

"Won't be long before you'll be taking him out of there," Zelda said. "He's already starting to try out those legs. I think what we might do, we might shut off a corner of the kitchen with a fence arrangement, put newspapers down and let him get the feel of it. Or maybe in the yard, now that it's getting warmer—"

A sharp knock at the back door made them both look toward it. "Come on in!" Zelda called out.

The door was pushed open and Leslie Harte stuck her head in, large sunglasses pushed onto the top of her head.

"Hi, everybody," she called out cheerily. "Sorry to barge in on you so early, but I was looking for Jake next door and couldn't find him. Any idea where he's gone?"

"Probably out on a call," Zelda said. "He doesn't keep me informed. Come on in, Leslie. Have some coffee."

"Oh . . . well, maybe just for a minute. I'm sure he'll be along soon—we have a date this morning."

"Here, Leslie," Hannah said, getting up and producing another coffee cup, keeping her voice even in spite of the flip-flops she was feeling inside. Leslie was looking fresh and radiant in one of her creamy silk shirts and a linen skirt in a vivid melon color. She was carrying a rolled-up sheaf of papers in one hand, her slim fingers curled around it, every nail varnished soft pink.

"What kind of date?" Zelda asked with a frank lack of inhibition. She poured coffee for Leslie, who seated herself in the chair opposite Hannah's and shook her head at the offer of toast.

"We're going to drive out the Dudley Pond road—you know, the one that hooks up with the interstate." Hannah got the distinct impression that she was delighted to be asked.

"What's out there?" Zelda frowned.

"Well, for one thing, a perfectly wonderful piece of property that Daddy just heard about recently. Part of the old Tarbell farm?"

"Oh, yes. I remember that. Mamie Tarbell and I went to school together."

"It's going on the market shortly, and I absolutely insisted that Jake see it because of the great location."

"Location for what?" Hannah asked cautiously, feeling a chill of apprehension.

"Why, the new animal clinic and boarding kennel Jake's going to build—if I can just convince him he should." Leslie's voice trailed off into a delighted laugh. "Actually, I think I'm more than halfway there on the convincing part, and when he sees this property, that ought to do it. It's a beautiful spot, and so close to the interstate that it would open up a much bigger practice for him."

"That what he wants, you think? A bigger practice?" Zelda asked.

"I'm not sure he knows it—not yet, anyway," Leslie replied, growing serious. "But anybody with his talent and ability shouldn't confine himself to the narrow scope of a country practice. And another wonderful thing about this property is that there's plenty of room for a house, as well. Much better to have the house separate from the practice—and he'll have all the best equipment. Well, look...this will give you an idea." She unrolled the papers she'd been carrying and spread them on the table.

"I had a friend of Daddy's from Albany make up some preliminary sketches. He's an architect, and when I explained what was needed, he came up with some great ideas. Jake hasn't seen them yet...."

She weighted the drawings down with sugar bowl and cups and pointed a shell-pink nail at them. Hannah, looking through a sudden blur, saw vague outlines of a sleek professional building, and, at a distance, an elegant multilevel home with arched mullioned windows, stone steps and cantilevered decks.

"This is just a rough sketch to show how the buildings would fit on the property," Leslie explained. "He's also done breakdowns of interiors and so on, but this gives you the general idea."

"Doesn't look as if Jake's present clients would be allowed inside that place," Zelda observed acidly.

"Oh, Zelda, you are the limit!" Leslie trilled good-naturedly. "Why, he'd have much better treatment facilities than he has now in that old house of his."

"Some of us *like* old houses," Zelda snapped.

"Oh, sorry...you know I didn't mean anything. But a professional man should keep up with the latest trends and developments. That's the part of the whole plan I know will really appeal to Jake."

Zelda didn't answer, and Hannah found it impossible to speak. Leslie, not at all perturbed, rolled up the sketches again and took a sip of coffee. "Well, I must run. Jake's probably back by now. Lovely to see you both. Hannah, my brother's going to be in touch with you shortly. He's longing to have you come along on our hunt-club working party next week."

"Oh? Well, we'll see..." Hannah said lamely, and Zelda got up and opened the door for Leslie as if, Hannah thought, to speed her on her way. When she had left in a flurry of goodbyes and expensive scent, Zelda returned slowly to the table and sat down.

Hannah felt cold with dismay and at the same time surprised at the depth of her pain. How little she knew of Jake's life, and how little he seemed to want her to know! He'd never uttered a word to her of these plans. After all this time, all these days when she had begun to feel more and more at home in Harrison Falls, she was suddenly a complete outsider again.

As if reading her mind, Zelda said bluntly, "Well, that was news to me."

"It certainly looks... ambitious," Hannah managed to stammer.

Zelda nodded but didn't speak again for several minutes. Both of them sipped their coffee. The toast grew cold, untouched.

"You know that Mamie Tarbell I mentioned before—girl I went to school with? She was a lot like Leslie."

"How?"

"Oh, you know—every curl in place. Her mother made those curls in the morning before she sent her to school. And Mamie was never mussed-up, never dirty. Never skinned her knees even. Me, I always had scabby knees and the hem out of my dress. It got so I finally couldn't stand it any longer."

"And?" Hannah rested her chin on one hand and looked across at Zelda.

"I put a garter snake down her back."

In spite of herself, Hannah laughed. "Well, I hope you're not thinking of doing *that* to Leslie." She glanced away from Zelda, across the room, out through the window where the branch of a pine moved against the glass. "She certainly is beautiful."

"So was Mamie Tarbell," Zelda said.

Hannah looked down at the tablecloth. A novelty, that was all she was to Jake. Coming from the city, wide-eyed at country life, she was an amusement to him. No one to be taken seriously, no one to confide in about important plans. No one, certainly, to compete with Leslie Harte. And how well Leslie knew him. How accurately she had zeroed in on the one thing that would appeal to him—his professional pride, his longing to do the very best for his clients. Very well, then, that settled it, Hannah thought coldly. Whatever there had been between Jake and her—and it was little enough—would go no further.

"Of course it does sound like Leslie's plan more than his," Zelda suggested.

"Don't worry, he'll go for it," Hannah said. The bitterness in her own voice sounded harsh to her.

She hesitated only briefly when Walker Harrison called later to invite her to the hunt-club event. "Are you sure I wouldn't be in the way?" she asked apprehensively. "It sounds like serious business—a working party."

"Anything but. It's always fun. Everybody brings clippers and pruning saws and a couple of pickups go along with us to collect the trash. Trails get overgrown from one year to the next, and also this year we're cutting a couple of new ones. Hunt season'll be here before you know it. But I promise you won't have to do anything but look beautiful—which for you is no trouble at all."

She ignored the compliment. "What about riding? Isn't that involved? I mean, I had a pony one summer, light-years ago at my grandfather's house, but that hardly counts, does it?"

"I'll give you a nice gentle horse and a couple of pointers on staying in the saddle. That's all you'll need."

"Could I have Lady's Maid?" she asked on sudden inspiration.

"She'd be a perfect choice."

"Well, then, okay. But I'll get myself there this time. You'll have your hands full, I'm sure."

"If that suits you. I usually spend some time at the office Saturday morning, so it would be a help."

As she hung up, Hannah thought that it wouldn't be difficult to avoid Jake McCabe for the next few days. If she did see him at the hunt-club affair on the weekend, Leslie would be an inhibiting presence between them. She called up reserves of self-control and began planning her next "country life" article for Bob Anderson.

THIS GATHERING of the hunt club was in marked contrast to the last one. As Hannah drove up the approach to the Harrison's home early on Saturday, she could see that those already assembled were in jeans, jodhpurs, boots, sweatshirts—every sort of informal down-to-work apparel. Peyton Harrison was in a well-worn pair of trousers that looked as if they'd seen a hundred fishing trips. On his head was a mashed-down white cotton hat that also appeared to be a veteran of hard wear. Walker, like most of the men, was in jeans and boots. Leslie managed to lend a high-fashion look to the occasion in her slim jeans, high-laced field boots and sleeveless riding blouse with mandarin collar. Oh, well, Hannah thought, it was probably last season's blouse. Then at once she scolded herself for being snide. This was Leslie's turf, after all, and it was nice of them to have invited her.

She lingered for a time in the stable yard, chatting with Peyton Harrison and greeting others she'd met at the earlier party. Bethany Harte, looking more like an ordinary thirteen-year-old today in denims and T-shirt, greeted her with perfunctory politeness—not much improvement there, Hannah thought—and asked if Jake and Carrie would be coming soon.

"I've no idea," Hannah said. She thought Bethany might be curious about Carrie's new horse, which she would surely have heard about by now. And moments later when the Jeep pulled up with a horse trailer in tow, she saw Bethany come alert. Hannah managed to work herself around to the other side of a small knot of bystanders so that she was partly out of sight. But she couldn't resist peeking, and her heart experienced a painful turnover as she saw Jake slide out and go around to help Carrie unload Foxfire. With an effort of will she forced herself to look away, and it was then that she caught the look on Bethany's face as she stood staring at the two of them, watching as they laughed and coaxed the mare out. Jealousy she would have expected, Hannah told herself. Or bitterness. Even animosity. But what she saw in the girl's face was something Hannah knew and recognized at once. Something she knew all about. Loneliness.

"I'm going to bring Lady's Maid out for you now, Hannah," Walker said, appearing at her elbow. "We'll be ready to ride out in a couple of minutes."

"Oh, dear. Will I be able to stay on?" Hannah asked apprehensively. "I've never had a real riding lesson."

"Certainly. Wait right here." He put an arm across her shoulders and gave her an encouraging squeeze, then hurried off toward the stable. Cautiously Hannah glanced back at the recent arrivals. Foxfire was out of the trailer and Carrie was throwing a saddle across her back. Bethany sauntered over.

"Will your horse be all right on the trails, do you think?" Hannah heard her ask. "I'm not taking Major. He's too sensitive and high-strung for that kind of riding. I'm going on Misty."

"Foxfire will go anywhere," Carrie said simply. "She's just wonderful."

Bethany gave an indifferent shrug but then added, a little tentatively, Hannah thought, "We could ride out together—if you want to, that is."

"Oh, I'd like that, Bethany," Carrie said, smiling.

"I'll be leaving now," Peyton Harrison said, and Hannah turned to him quickly. "I'm going to ride in one of the pickups—privilege of age. But don't worry about Lady's Maid tossing you. She's as gentle as a lamb."

"Exactly what I need." Hannah laughed, waving him off. Others in the group were getting on their mounts now and she was left in plain sight as she waited for Walker to return. Jake strolled over to her.

"Haven't seen much of you lately. Where have you been keeping yourself?" His blue eyes probed her face as he looked down at her. His mouth, framing a smile, gave Hannah a moment's pang as she recalled the strength and softness of those lips on hers only a few nights ago. She pulled herself together and said casually, "Right where I've been all along—up in my room working away. Just haven't had time for anything else. Besides, you must be pretty busy yourself, aren't you? With plans for the new clinic?"

He looked startled. "New clinic? Oh...that. Well, nothing's been decided really—"

"But it will be soon, won't it?" a voice chimed in, and Leslie appeared leading two horses. Her smile radiated self-confidence.

Jake had collected himself and was back to his easy-going posture. "Leslie and her plans," he said with tolerant good humor. "There's no stopping her." It seemed to Hannah the exasperation was only token. There was more affection than annoyance there, she was sure.

"Here you are, darling," Leslie said. "I had Clipper saddled for you." She turned to Hannah. "He's one of our biggest horses. We're putting Jake in charge of the high branches. Come on, Jake, you and I will lead out. Walker's just coming with your horse, Hannah. Hope you have fun."

Hannah gave a little wave of her hand as the two of them swung smoothly onto their horses and rode off. Jake cast her a curious, lingering look over his shoulder, but then Leslie leaned toward him and said something, reclaiming his attention.

Walker appeared at the same moment with Lady's Maid, and Hannah was obliged to give him her complete concentration.

"Left foot in the stirrup to mount," he ordered, and then, when she swung up into the saddle, "Well! You did that beautifully. I think you're going to be a quick learner. All right, let me adjust the length of these for you." He fussed with the stirrups, giving her instructions as he did so. "Keep your heels down, toes up. And hold the horse with your knees. Makes both of you feel more secure. Reins in the right hand, left hand free. Gentle pressure to guide her—no quick jerks. Lady's a great little horse. You won't have any trouble with her. Just nudge her with your heels to get her going."

Well, thought Hannah, *here goes*. Heart beating fast, she poked Lady's Maid gently with her heels and the horse started off sedately after the other riders.

There were, as nearly as Hannah could count, between fifteen and twenty riders in the party. They rode out of the fenced pasture and over the rolling hills and wooded slopes of the Harrison property. Two four-wheel-drive pickups went on ahead, one of them carrying chain saws and pruning hooks. Peyton Harrison waved to her from the front seat of the first one, and Hannah, feeling more secure than she had anticipated, waved back with her free hand. Once she'd decided she wasn't going to fall off, she begged Walker, who had been sticking close beside her, to go on ahead with the others.

"I'm not a bit afraid," she insisted. "They'll be needing you to help up front. I'll just follow along and enjoy the scenery."

"You're sure?" He leaned toward her and put a hand on her arm.

"Absolutely. Lady's Maid and I are two of a kind. We'll get along fine."

"Okay. But I'll be checking back with you." He smiled encouragingly and trotted off after the rest of the group.

Hannah watched him go, then gave Lady's Maid a cautious prod with her heels. The horse obediently broke into a gentle trot that brought Hannah closer to the main party. She could observe them plainly now and picked out Jake at once, since he was the tallest rider. As they entered a wooded area she saw him reach up and begin pruning branches overhead, guiding his horse skillfully so that by the time the branches fell both he and the horse were in the clear. Staying close to him, Leslie rode easily and well, Hannah saw. She reached out from time to time with a pair of long-handled clippers to trim back small branches, and she leaned toward him frequently, commenting, pointing, laughing. Hannah swallowed painfully, then wrenched her eyes away and looked for the two girls.

Bethany and Carrie were still riding close together, and each of them carried small pruning shears with which they cut back twigs and brambles. Novice though she was, Hannah could readily see Foxfire's sturdy gait and quick response to command as Carrie led her through the overgrown thickets. "She's just wonderful," Carrie had said to Bethany, and Hannah had heard the pride in her voice.

The sun rose higher and the group worked its way in and out of brush, over hills, into woods and out again. Voices called back and forth, orders were shouted, laughter rang out, and now and again the morning quiet was stabbed by the whine of a power saw as a tree or large branch was cut. Walker rode back to check on Hannah repeatedly.

"Getting hungry?" he asked late in the morning. "There's food in one of the trucks. We'll all be stopping in another hour or so."

"Please don't worry about me." Hannah laughed. "Lady's Maid and I are getting along beautifully. I didn't know it would be so much fun." And surprisingly it was. The warm summer air felt soft against her face and she would have enjoyed herself thoroughly if she could have avoided those frequent glimpses of Jake and Leslie together. Still, she told herself with stern logic, that was something she was going to have to get used to for her remaining time in Harrison Falls. Better to face it and deal with it. She turned her thinking to a story she would write for the paper tonight—a novice rider on her first day in the saddle.

Then, piercing the morning's serenity, came a sudden shriek from a horse. Lady's Maid shied and whinnied and took several nervous steps sideways. Instinctively Hannah tightened her knees around the horse's sides, patted her and spoke reassuringly. At once the mare grew quieter, although her eyes rolled anxiously and she stood quite still, reluctant to move. Hannah shaded her eyes, peering up ahead to where the main group was working. Then she saw that Bethany had jumped down and was quieting her own horse, Misty, who had a gash across her chest that was bleeding profusely. A big branch lopped from one of the trees lay in the path, ready to be picked up. The horse had apparently stepped on it, thrusting it upward, and the sharp end must have raked her.

Carrie cupped her hands to her mouth and called out to Jake, who was riding ahead of them. "Dad! Over here! Quick!"

Hannah saw Jake gallop back, followed by Leslie. He slid out of the saddle and walked quickly to the injured animal. Leslie dismounted and ran after him, and the two of them looked with concern at the cut.

"That's going to have to be sutured, isn't it?" she heard Leslie say.

"It is, yes, though I don't think it's deep. But she'll need antibiotics and a tetanus shot, too. Look, I've got all the stuff in my car. I'll lead her back with me and take care of it. You go on with the group. I'll rejoin you as soon as I've fixed her up."

Leslie nodded agreement and Bethany, still slightly pale, said, "I'll walk back and pick up another horse."

"I'll take you," Carrie offered. "We can ride double on Foxfire. Come on."

"Good idea," Jake said, and as Hannah watched, the procession set off for the house, Jake on the big horse Clipper leading the injured Misty, the two girls following. Bethany rode behind Carrie, her arms around the other girl's waist. Walker had joined the group, and when he rode over to Hannah, she was quick to assure him she was fine.

"Just get back to work and forget about me," she said. "I'm getting braver by the minute. Only maybe I'll stay back a little farther. Lady's Maid seems to like peace and quiet. I saw her ears go back when those power saws started up."

"If you stay in town long enough we'll have you riding out with us this fall," Walker promised. He gave her a lingering look before wheeling his horse around. Hannah waved him off and waited for the group to move on, then spoke some words of encouragement to Lady's Maid, nudging her once more with her heels. The incident past, the horse returned to her former steady gait and moved on with total unconcern. Hannah shook her head with admiration. "Wish I had your emotional makeup, old girl," she sighed.

Well behind the other riders a few minutes later, Hannah spotted an alternate trail leading off to the left, and on an impulse coaxed her horse into it. She was feeling more confident in the saddle now, more comfortable with the good-natured mare. The bright June morning seemed to invite exploration, and the little tree-shaded path beckoned with its sun-dappled curves and gentle rise. She would go a short distance along it, then

turn and rejoin the others, she decided. Lady's Maid
seemed to fall in with the idea and moved along at a
gentle trot that slowed to a walk as the slope grew
steeper. They went in and out of the trees, across grassy
stretches, always keeping to the trail, and presently
Hannah realized she could no longer hear the sound of
the main group. She probably shouldn't have gone so far
on her own, she thought, but she felt quite at ease and
happy, even though the trail was beginning to show signs
of becoming overgrown on this higher level. Only a little farther, just to see where it would lead, she told herself, and then she'd return.

But the way wound on and on, higher and higher, and
after a time Hannah decided reluctantly that she should
turn back. She almost regretted the need to, for she was
feeling confident and capable out here on her own. And
the prospect of Jake's return and Leslie's hovering pro-
prietary air with him was not something she looked forward to.

Lady's Maid had just climbed over a rise where a large
flat tract of open land stretched out before them. Hannah, pulling on the reins and preparing to turn the horse
back, glanced at it and then took a second look. For
several moments she stared at it, frowning. This piece of
land was in sharp contrast to the unspoiled meadows and
woods she'd just passed through. Here the ground was
bare and bulldozed, scarred with heavy tire tracks. It had
a bleak, ravaged look. Slowly Hannah dismounted and
let the reins drop from her hand. She crept up closer to
the edge of the wasted expanse and stared, her mind
working rapidly but futilely as she tried to figure it out.
She assumed she was still on Harrison land. If so, what
conceivable purpose could this tract serve? For some
time she stood there puzzling over it. An inkling of an

idea nudged her mind, but just as she prepared to examine it, explore it further, she heard a whinnying sound from some distance away and turned to look for Lady's Maid.

"Oh, gosh!" Hannah began to hurry down the sloping trail, pushing aside brambles, berry bushes and saplings as she located the mare, who was ambling back on her own, ducking her head every now and then to tear off tempting bits of greenery along the path. She was already thirty or forty yards away.

"Lady! Wait up, Lady!" Hannah called out, but the next moment she heard hoofbeats and she saw Lady's Maid lift her head curiously as another horse came trotting up the old trail. Hannah's breath caught painfully as she saw Jake ride up on Clipper, the big powerful horse taking the hill without apparent effort.

He spotted Lady's Maid, and she saw his glance dart anxiously along the path until he saw her. Then he got down and hurried over to her.

"I thought for a minute you'd been thrown," he said lightly. "That would have been a first for sure, with Lady. Are you okay?" His arm had slipped around her, but Hannah thought that was only a gesture of reassurance. She stiffened and pulled back.

"Yes, of course. I'm fine. I got off to look around and forgot to tie my horse. I suppose that's what I should have done."

"With Lady, definitely. You're lucky she didn't trot all the way home to the barn and leave you stranded."

"Oh, I guess I could have walked," Hannah said, but she could feel how forced her smile was. "How's Bethany's horse?"

"All patched up, and none the worse for it, I'm sure. The girls are already back with the group." He turned to catch her horse's reins and now held both animals.

"Hannah, why are you avoiding me?" he asked quietly.

She felt her face flushing with anger. "I didn't know I was."

"I thought we were friends."

"Friends? Well, that depends on the definition, I suppose." She brushed past him on the narrow trail, ready to mount her horse.

"What does that mean?" His forehead had drawn together in a frown that darkened his features.

"Just that I began to feel I was encroaching on somebody else's private preserve. That's not something I do."

"And besides, Walker Harrison's more your type, isn't he?" His mouth curved in a bitter half smile.

The flush on Hannah's face deepened. "That's right—turn the whole thing around so it becomes my fault. Much easier on your conscience that way, isn't it?"

"I'm not turning anything around," he snapped. "I'm merely pointing out—"

"Well, let me tell you something." Hannah stuck one foot in the stirrup. "Just a bit of advice. Next time you decide to come on to the new girl in town, make sure she's someone who can't see through you, Dr. McCabe." She swung up into the saddle. "It'll work out better."

He handed her the reins, avoiding a direct look at her. His face was a pale mask of fury. She guided the mare down the trail and nudged her with her heels. Stepping carefully but more quickly than she had on the way up,

Lady's Maid headed back the way they'd come. Hannah could hear the heavy measured thud of Clipper's hooves behind her as Jake followed, but it was almost drowned out by the angry pounding of her heart.

CHAPTER SEVEN

HULLING STRAWBERRIES in Zelda's kitchen, Hannah glanced down at the puppy, who was starting to take a few tottering steps on his own. His sides were already looking sleekly rounded, and he trailed after her wherever she went now. She smiled at his efforts and went on with her work as the berries stained her fingertips bright red. Outside the open window, the pine brushed against the screen, and beyond, Zelda's roses, a mass of June blossoms, sent their fragrance into the house.

"Zelda?" The back door was pushed open tentatively and Carrie McCabe stuck her head in.

"Hi, Carrie. Zelda isn't here. Have a strawberry."

"Oh, gosh. Where is she?" The girl's freckled face looked distressed.

"In the village. She took the truck in to have the brakes worked on. She was going over to the church to help set up tables for the strawberry festival while she waited."

"Oh, gosh," Carrie said again.

"Something wrong?"

Carrie came in, swung Sam up into her arms and sat down at the table, all in one movement.

"Well, not really wrong, but the Rittenmyers think there is, and Mrs. Rittenmyer's scared and I said I'd come and help. But I need Zelda and the truck because my dad's out on calls."

Once again Hannah felt as though she were in a foreign country, hearing the natives speak a language she couldn't understand.

"What does all that mean?" she asked.

"There's a swarm of bees over at the Rittenmyers' place," the girl explained patiently. "They've lit on a low branch of the dogwood right outside the kitchen door, and Mrs. Rittenmyer's scared to go in or out. I said I'd come and get them."

"Are they your bees?"

Carrie stroked Sam's head. "Well, they might be. Or they could be wild ones. I don't know. But I said I'd coax them off the tree for her, anyway, and now I don't know how to manage."

"Can you do that?" Hannah asked.

"Oh, sure. It's no trick. People get scared when they see a swarm like that—"

"So would I."

"Yes, but see, the thing is—" Carrie reached for a strawberry and popped it in her mouth "—they've left their old hive. Probably a queen led them out and they're looking for a new place. They've got scouts out right now trying to find one. But they don't feel any territorial loyalty to that dogwood branch, so they won't defend it. No stings, in other words."

"Well, thank goodness for that."

"But people don't believe it when I tell them. Like Mrs. Rittenmyer. So that's why I said I'd come and help."

"Couldn't I take you over there?" Hannah asked. "Do you have to take a lot of equipment? My car isn't very big, but—"

"Oh, would you, Hannah? That'd be great. All I have to take is one hive with some combs in it—it would fit in that little back seat of yours, I think."

"All right." Hannah was already moving to the sink to wash her hands. "I've finished these, anyway. Let me just write a quick note for Zelda. Put Sam over there in his pen. He won't like it, but he'll be all right."

Carrie put the puppy down gently behind the low barricade that had been erected in a corner for him. At once he started a pitiful whining. "Oh, my. Learning fast," Carrie said with a wise shake of her head.

"Okay, let's go," Hannah said, propping the note against the sugar bowl.

As they pulled out of the driveway, Hannah warned, "Don't expect me to participate in this business, now. In spite of that talk about no stings, I'm not up to facing several dozen bees."

Carrie gave her a sideways look. "Well, actually, there might be a few more than that."

"How many more?" Hannah asked nervously.

"Probably a few thousand, the way it sounded."

Hannah gulped and drove on. After a time Carrie said, "You know, your helping me with these bees— well, I'm kind of sorry it happened this way, because I was going to ask a favor of you, anyway, and now this makes two. Two favors, I mean."

"Goodness, we aren't keeping score, are we? What's the other one?"

"Well, school's out this week, and the honor society's going on a trip to Albany. To meet the governor and see stuff. Only it's overnight."

"And you get to go because you're honor society? Carrie, that's wonderful."

"Yeah, except I'm worried about Foxfire and who'd take care of her. I mean, my dad would do it, but he's awful busy and sometimes he gets back late from calls. So I thought if you could do it—just for that little time I'm away..."

The suggestion made Hannah vaguely uneasy. "Well, couldn't Tully?"

"Oh sure, I suppose. But I think Foxfire would like you better—that's really the reason I'm asking. And I'd feel better if I knew it was you. Only if you'd rather not, it's okay. I mean, I just thought it wouldn't hurt to ask."

Hannah felt suddenly touched. "Oh, Carrie, of course I'll do it," she said. No reason she couldn't run over and take care of the horse quietly and without seeing Jake. And what if she did see him? As things stood now what possible difference could it make to either of them?

MR. AND MRS. RITTENMYER, several neighbors and an assortment of children were gathered at a safe distance when the Porsche pulled up and Carrie unloaded her equipment. All of them greeted Hannah and Carrie warmly, but with a kind of desperation.

"Don't worry, Mrs. Rittenmyer," Carrie said. "They'll be gone in no time."

Hannah looked apprehensively at the tree where the mass of bees hung, weighing down the low branch so heavily that many of them were on the ground. She watched Carrie set the hive a short distance away. "I've put a comb in it that bees have already worked," Carrie explained to her. "These bees will smell it and go right toward it."

"Shouldn't you have worn your helmet and all that other stuff?" Hannah whispered.

"I told you, they won't sting. I could pick them up with my hands, only this is simpler. Now we have to watch for the queen. She'll be bigger than the others. The queen has to be there or it won't work. She has to enter the hive with them."

Hannah glanced at her, and an odd random thought struck her—how much Carrie's mother had given up when she turned her back on this girl!

It took a few minutes for the bees to catch the scent of the honeycomb. When they did they began a steady march toward it, and Carrie stood by watching carefully. Several minutes later, she let out a delighted cry. "There she is!" Hannah followed her pointing finger to see a bee larger than the rest—long and black and with three golden stripes—making her way toward the hive.

"It'll be all right now," Carrie said. "They'll all follow her in." She turned to the Rittenmyers and the other onlookers. "That's it—show's over." Hannah shook her head in wonder at such youthful aplomb and began framing in her mind the words to write it as a story.

The last of the long procession had straggled into the hive, and the little group of watchers had broken up when Zelda's pickup came roaring up the drive, with Zelda and Jake in it.

"Did we miss the whole thing?" Zelda called out as she slid to the ground.

"Situation under control," Hannah said proudly, feeling curiously as if she'd been a participant instead of merely a nervous onlooker. She kept her eyes averted from Jake, but she was intensely aware of his presence as he jumped down from the truck and strode over to join them.

"Sorry you had to be pressed into service," he said quietly, and Hannah, no longer able to avoid looking at him, managed a noncommittal smile. "Wouldn't have missed it," she replied pleasantly.

"This is one of Carrie's flashier acts." He grinned, and Hannah's heart gave a skip at the way his eyes crinkled at the corners. "I think really she enjoys doing it."

"Well, why not?" Zelda said. "Not many people would be willing to. They think it's the next thing to snake charming."

"Although it's all perfectly scientific and easy to understand once she explains it," Hannah said quickly.

Zelda glanced from Hannah to Jake and then toward Carrie, who was shoving a piece of screening over the entrance to the hive. "We'll put that in the truck," Zelda said, and Jake stepped forward to lift the hive, now heavy with its freight of bees. "Carrie, you and I had better take them back in the pickup and I'll help you set them up in the bee yard. Hannah, you could give Jake a lift home, couldn't you?"

Hannah threw Zelda a quick desperate look and tried to shake her head, but Zelda was already moving away, helping to let down the tailgate so the hive could be placed carefully on the truck bed. "Sure, why not?" Hannah murmured, but inside she was fuming silently.

"How about a truce?" he asked minutes later, glancing at her as they got into the Porsche. His long legs looked crowded in the low car.

Hannah turned the key in the ignition and backed slowly down the Rittenmyers' driveway. Both of them lifted their hands to wave at the family, who stood on the porch steps seeing them off.

"We're not at war, Dr. McCabe," she said, trying to sound lighthearted as she pulled out onto the road and headed toward home. The pickup was already out of sight ahead of them.

"You could've fooled me," he said, and in spite of herself, Hannah had to laugh. Yet her feelings were in a turmoil. Every time she was with him she found it harder to reconcile the Jake who was to marry Leslie—might as well say it, she scolded herself—with the Jake she'd thought she knew. It was as if he were two different men, one the impulsive, laughing stranger who had kissed her in the twilight at Carrie's birthday party, the other the smooth, correct professional man she'd twice seen at the Harrisons'. That man was bound by ties of long habit and association to life here in Harrison Falls. A life that included Leslie Harte, who, it was all too obvious, was more than willing to take all the details of planning for the future into her own capable hands. If she herself had been hurt along the way, Hannah thought, it was only because she'd broken her own first rule: don't get so close to people that they matter too much to you.

"...really has opened up to you," Jake was saying, and Hannah, quickly collecting her scattered thoughts, answered, "I'm sorry—what did you say?"

"I said, Carrie's really opened up to you since you've been here. She's never been able to have that kind of relationship with Joyce—her mother."

"How sad for both of them," Hannah murmured.

"I think Joyce would like to improve the situation— a little belatedly, it's true. She's invited Carrie to California this summer for a visit. But Carrie's dug in her heels and says no. She can be pretty determined when she wants to be. I'd certainly have no objection if Carrie wanted to visit her mother now and then. Might even be a good thing."

"Maybe Joyce is beginning to realize how much she's missing, never seeing her daughter," Hannah said, remembering how this thought had occurred to her, too.

"I suppose that would be natural."

"It can't have been easy for you, raising a child all by yourself."

"A good many women do it."

"Yes, that's true. And I'm sure it's not easy for them, either."

The Porsche hummed along the narrow county road and turned into Jake's driveway.

"Carrie's asked me to take care of Foxfire when she goes on the trip to Albany," Hannah said casually, bringing the car to a stop but not turning off the engine.

"Has she? Please don't feel you have to."

"She seemed to think you'd be pretty busy. And I don't mind at all. Only I'm counting on her to give me the right instructions."

He nodded, and the silence between them throbbed with unspoken words, suppressed feelings. He was giving her a long steady look, blue eyes seeking, probing, trying to read something, Hannah thought. She slid her gaze away and said briskly, "Well! That was quite an adventure. I'd better dash now—strawberry festival at the church tonight."

"Getting used to the mad social whirl here in Harrison Falls?" he asked with a twinkle.

"That's not quite as funny as it sounds," she said. "Zelda manages to keep things boiling all the time."

He got out of the car and hesitated for only a moment before striding off toward the house with a wave of his hand. Hannah's fingers gripped the wheel so hard she had to make a conscious effort to unclench them as she turned the car around.

"ABOUT THIS MUCH," Carrie demonstrated, scooping sweet-feed out of a big barrel in the stable. "And fresh water, of course. She can go out in the pasture in the morning. In the evening I fill a hay net for her—see this thing?" She pointed to a limp mesh bag hanging in Foxfire's stall. "Hay's over here." She led Hannah to a corner of the shed where bales were stacked and where loose hay was spread thickly over the floor.

"What about cleaning her stall?"

"Well, yes. Are you sure you're not going to mind?" Carrie's eyebrows drew together worriedly.

"No, of course not. What do I use? That thing?" Hannah pointed at a fork hanging against one wall.

"Yes, and then spread some fresh straw."

"Sounds simple. I know I won't have a bit of trouble. You just forget about everything and have a wonderful time."

Subject matter was piling up, Hannah thought with wry amusement as she hurried back home to finish her articles on bee management and the strawberry festival. And if she played her cards right she could arrange to duck across to the stable and take care of Foxfire without ever running into Jake.

The weather took a gloomy turn that week as the skies clouded over and the air became heavy, oppressive.

"Something building," Zelda said with a knowing nod toward the clouds that loomed on the horizon. All day they'd been hearing rumbles of distant thunder, but there was still no rain. Carrie's bus had left early for Albany, and Hannah had felt the close, heavy air around her when she went next door to feed Foxfire, lead her out into the pasture, then return to muck out the stall. Even so, the work had been satisfying, and the fresh stall was as pleasant to contemplate as a scrubbed kitchen. From the direction of the house she could hear Tully banging around as he cleaned the kennels and put things to rights for the day's office hours. She hurried home quickly before Jake returned from his early-morning calls.

She and Zelda carried their lunch—sandwiches and iced tea—out to the front porch at noon to take advantage of whatever small vagrant breeze there might be, but the heat pressed closer around them hour by hour, and presently there seemed to be no air moving at all.

"I've got a good fan I'm going to put in your room," Zelda said decisively. "You'll need something if this doesn't break soon."

"I'll be all right," Hannah insisted, reflecting with some surprise that it was a long time since she'd thought about air-conditioning. The high-ceilinged rooms and shuttered windows here seemed to make it unnecessary.

"No, no, I'm going to give it to you. I know right where I put it—in that little storeroom off the kitchen. Once or twice every summer I have to pull it out." Zelda had changed from her habitual jeans and shirt into a loose housedress covered with big red poppies. Hannah's hair was caught up and skewered to the top of her head with pins to keep it off her neck, and she wore a sleeveless tank top with her denim skirt and sandals.

Sam frisked in his wobbly fashion around their feet, falling frequently and finally collapsing, lopsided and panting, against Hannah's leg. She reached down absentmindedly to scratch between his ears, then picked him up and held him on her lap, where he promptly fell asleep.

"Wonder how he's going to like city life," Zelda mused.

Hannah looked at her, startled. "Actually, I hadn't thought much about that." Or about anything else connected to her life in New York, she realized suddenly. It wasn't the first time this had occurred to her, yet she'd been going along from day to day with hardly a thought of the future. "I know I'll miss him, but I always picture him staying here. Not that I want to saddle you with him...."

"Oh, shoot." Zelda's hand waved her off. "I'll take him, and gladly. Only he'll be lonesome for you. Animals always know who they belong to."

"I'm sure he'll get over it," Hannah said a little dryly. She gave Zelda a hesitant smile. "It would be nice, in a way, to be that certain about things. Knowing just where you belong and who you belong to..." Her voice trailed off and she looked away.

"Oh, I don't know," Zelda said. "A little uncertainty keeps things interesting. What do you think of Jake McCabe?" she asked suddenly.

Hannah could feel the sudden flush of color in her cheeks. "What about him?" she demanded.

"I just wondered how you felt about him."

"I don't feel... any way at all about him. I mean, nothing special. He's very nice and very much promised to Leslie Harte, I gather."

Zelda rose and began to pick up plates and glasses. "That's how it looks to you, does it?"

"And to the whole town, I imagine."

"Oh, well, yes." She headed for the door, then glanced back over her shoulder. "Of course this town's been fooled before." She chuckled and went into the house.

HANNAH SPENT MOST of the afternoon in her room working on the story about Carrie and the swarming bees. Since sending the first articles to Bob Anderson she had averaged two a week, and his last note, written diagonally across the sheet of a memo pad in his familiar scrawl, urged, "Send more. Could use 3 a wk."

All the windows were open, curtains hanging limp. The fan Zelda had brought up from the storeroom whirred energetically but scarcely budged the solid mass of humid air, which seemed a tangible presence in the room. The puppy, curled up on a thick bath towel near the table where Hannah worked, slept soundly, now and then making small sighing noises and stretching out his toes.

Late in the afternoon Hannah finished the piece she was working on, kicked off her sandals and sank down on the bed. From somewhere far distant she could hear mutterings of thunder. She listened to them for a time. Then they grew fainter as she dozed off.

She was awakened by the sound of hurried footsteps. Zelda came bustling into the room and headed straight for the windows, which she began slamming down. Wind was sweeping into the room, blowing the curtains and bringing moisture with it. Lightning streaked the sky and a shattering clap of thunder followed it.

"Sorry to barge in and disturb you," Zelda said. "But you didn't hear my knock and I thought you'd get soaked in here."

Hannah was scrambling out of bed and pulling on her sandals. "What time is it? How long did I sleep?"

"It's pretty close to six," Zelda said.

"Foxfire!" Hannah cried. "Oh, gosh, she's out in the pasture. I've got to go get her."

"That pasture connects with the rear of the stable, doesn't it?" Zelda said. "Isn't there an overhang there? I bet she's got herself home and is just fine. Anyway, somebody's probably already taken care of her."

"But I was supposed to—it was my responsibility!" Hannah wailed. "And what if she's scared of all the thunder and lightning? Horses are sensitive to things like that, aren't they?"

"Well, maybe some are. Foxfire looks pretty steady to me. And shoot, a little wet doesn't hurt a horse—wait now, where are you going? Take my old raincoat, it's by the front door—"

But Hannah was already out of the room and flying downstairs. Ignoring the raincoat Zelda had urged on her, she dashed out the front door and across the porch, down the steps and onto the familiar path toward the house next door. Rain was coming down hard, driven by an unrelenting wind. Lightning split the sky and thunder came rolling after it. The branches of the big trees in Zelda's yard bucked and swayed with the fury of the storm. The path underfoot was slick, and Hannah had to watch her footing as she ran. The hedge, heavy with rain, was bent down so that she had to force it back with her hands to get through. Water splattered against her and the twigs scratched her arms; she was already soaked from the downpour itself. Her tank top clung to her body, and her denim skirt was plastered against her legs.

She dashed into the shed that had been converted into Foxfire's stable and picked up one of the soft nylon lead ropes that hung on a hook by the door. Then she hurried around to the fenced area at the side, opening the gate and looking frantically for the little mare. And just as Zelda had predicted, there under the shed's broad overhang, stood Foxfire. In the wild noise of the storm, she seemed unhappy but none the worse for the experience.

"Oh, Foxy!" Hannah ran to the horse and threw her arms around her in a rush of relief. "What a smart girl you were to find shelter. Now come on. We'll go inside and give you your supper.'' She threw the lead rope over the horse's head, coaxing her gently out into the rain, through the gate and into the stable.

Once inside, Hannah removed the lead rope, and Foxfire trotted happily into her stall. Hannah looked for something to dry her with and spotted an old towel hanging on a nail. Zelda had said a little rain did a horse no harm, but was she just trying to be comforting? Did horses catch colds? Hannah rubbed the mare briskly with the towel, and now Foxfire showed the smallest sign of impatience, stamping one foot and tossing her head, obviously wondering why supper was such a long time appearing. At last Hannah felt reassured that she was sufficiently dry, so she tossed the towel aside and went to measure out the feed. Walking back and forth, filling the feed box and bringing fresh water, she felt a quiet comfort taking the place of her earlier anxiety. She glanced around at the worn wooden floor, smelled the sweetness of the hay, and thought what a lucky horse Foxfire was to have this good home to return to every night. Then her eyes fell on a jacket hanging on a peg against one wall. She walked slowly over and touched it gingerly. A waterproof jacket with a hood, well-worn and comfortable-looking. She ran her hand along one sleeve and felt a strange tingling sensation at the real-ization that this was Jake's coat, and that he must have casually reached for it a hundred times. It knew the curves and angles of his body well, had even shaped it-self to conform to them. Impulsively she put her cheek against it and smelled the clean male scent she associ-ated with him.

She moved reluctantly away and returned to the stall, taking the hay net from its hook and heading for the far corner of the shed where the hay was stored. Outside she could hear the roaring and pounding of the storm. Through the small window she saw lightning crack across the sky, then heard a booming roll of thunder. At the same moment the shed door burst open and Jake stood there, breathless and looking anxious. His hair was plastered wetly against his head and his denim shirt was soaked through. He glanced at Foxfire, now munching contentedly in her stall. Then he looked around the shed until he found Hannah, standing quietly in the dim corner by the hay bales. For a moment his eyes moved over her, taking in the wet tank top clinging to her breasts, the wet hair struggling loose from its pins.

"I was . . . worried about the horse," he said. "I was late getting home and I thought she might still be out in the pasture. I'm sure it wouldn't have hurt her, but—"

"I told Carrie I'd take care of her," Hannah said quietly. She stood motionless with the net in her hands, staring at him, feeling a curious suspension of time there in the dimness of the shed.

"It was just that the storm was so bad, I thought it might have kept you from coming over." He hesitated, and a gradual smile placed the look of concern he'd been wearing. "But yes, you did tell Carrie you'd look after her. And of course I should have known you would, Hannah Chase."

He crossed the shed slowly and stood in front of her.

"I was just going to fill this," Hannah stammered. Her heart had started a wild pounding and her voice seemed to have disappeared. The moment stretched out between them as his eyes drank her in.

"Hannah . . ." he whispered. Then, before she could move or think of another word to say, he had pulled her close to him and his strong arms were around her, locking her body against his. His mouth was on hers in a kiss that was more than the other kisses had been—more than questing, more than tender. Demanding, this time, and urgent, sweeping everything before it. Hannah felt enveloped, consumed by his passion. When at last she drew back, breathless, she tried to speak. "You don't . . . it's not right . . . we can't . . ."

"Why not?" he insisted. "Hannah, you can't say you haven't felt it, too."

"You hardly know me," she managed to whisper.

"I feel I've always known you," he murmured.

"But you haven't, really. And don't you see how wrong all this is?"

"It seems very right to me," he said in a low tense voice, smothering her objections with another kiss. Hannah felt her defenses crumbling away like sand before an incoming tide.

"I think I've loved you from the minute I saw you crashing through that hedge and getting stung by a bee. Right here . . ." His lips touched the spot.

"But you belong to Leslie! You're going to live in that new house she's planning, you're going to have that big practice—"

"There's not going to be any new house, and the practice I have now suits me just fine. Those things are all Leslie's ideas, not mine. I've tried to tell her so a dozen times, but she's unstoppable."

"But Leslie herself—you and she have an understanding."

"We have nothing of the sort!" His voice rose slightly in exasperation. "I've tried to tell her that, too. I think the whole town expects it now, the way she's been acting, but it isn't going to be. Don't you believe me?"

"It just seemed to me when we all rode out with the hunt club, you and she—"

"I wanted to explain things to you that very day, only you were there with Walker. And when I rode after you and finally did find you alone you wouldn't talk to me."

A slow smile curved Hannah's lips. "No, I guess I wouldn't. It was just that I thought—" She broke off and looked up at him, studying the direct sincerity in his blue eyes. "I thought it was so impossible. Not just because of Leslie, but because we don't live in the same world. I mean, people can't just put all those differences behind them."

"Can't they?" His voice was a whisper again. "People can do whatever they decide is right for them, it seems to me. And we're right for each other, Hannah."

"You don't know that," Hannah murmured back, struggling hard for reason and sanity. But inside all her emotions were bubbling and boiling, churning wildly as the meaning of what he was saying came home to her. He loved her! But what of all her stern self-discipline? What about keeping her distance, not letting love get too close?

"Hannah..." His voice came again, a soft caress, heavy with love. She lifted her face to him and his hands found her still-wet hair, pulling out the pins and letting it fall to her shoulders. He kissed her again, pressing her damp body so close she could feel the buttons of his shirt, the strength of his body, the shape of his very bones. She wanted it to last forever, this feeling of warmth and belonging, this passion that satisfied a hunger deep inside her.

Lightning flashed again and thunder exploded almost directly overhead. Rain pounded on the roof with renewed ferocity, but Hannah felt suddenly warm and

safe, sheltered as she had never been before. She let the
hay net drop from her hand as she slid her arms around
his neck and returned his kiss, letting her own desire
match his, closing her eyes and mind and heart to every
argument but love. Slowly they sank to the floor, where
the hay was soft and fragrant and blanketed the boards
in a sweet, thick layer that smelled of summer fields.
Skin next to skin as clothing fell away, they lay locked
together in wonder and discovery as the storm beat down
around them but failed to touch them.

CHAPTER EIGHT

BACK IN HER HIGH-CEILINGED room at Zelda Miles's house, Hannah woke just as dawn was creeping in grayly. The storm was over and the countryside lay washed and quiet. Hannah slipped out of bed, went to the window and threw it wide open. Clean cool air rushed in, moving her hair and bathing her face. She sank down on her knees at the low sill and rested her arms on it, watching for a long time as the light changed and the sun began to rise, turning the world to green and gold. How long was it since she'd been this happy, Hannah asked herself idly. Indeed, had she ever been so happy? Remembered words, caresses, ecstasies, flooded back over her as she relived the evening before, along with the memory of strong hands and demanding passion. But had it really been love? How could she know? Love should be something that had a meaning beyond today's passion, shouldn't it? It should be forever. Was that what she felt?

She entered the kitchen quietly, telling herself reassuringly that she looked the same as she did any other morning. Zelda was at the table with a confusion of papers spread in front of her, a pencil in her hand and reading glasses sliding down her nose. She glanced over the tops of the glasses at Hannah and said brightly, "Well! You certainly look smart and chipper this morning."

Hannah could feel herself blushing like a schoolgirl, wondering if her joyful mood was that obvious, but Zelda, appearing her usual matter-of-fact self, returned at once to her papers. "This thing gets more complicated every year," she grumbled.

"What is it?" Hannah asked, heading for the coffee maker.

"Annual Founder's Day picnic," Zelda sighed. "I'm on the committee. Just push those things aside and sit down. There's muffins on the counter."

Hannah split a muffin, buttered it and then sat gingerly at the table, taking care not to spill crumbs on the lists, notes and charts spread out there.

"When and where?" she inquired, glad to allow the conversation to drift away from herself.

"Next weekend down at the municipal park—you know, right across from the firehouse? That way, in case of rain they'll just move the fire truck out and we can have it inside. But it doesn't often rain on Founder's Day. Right now I'm sorting out the food. Who's to bring what and so on. We don't want to wind up with fourteen lemon jellies and only one potato salad—that sort of thing."

"Anything I can do to help?" Hannah took a bite of muffin and a sip of hot coffee. *He loves me,* a small voice in her head was singing. *He loves me.* "I could sort out some of these lists and copy them for you. Or anything else you might need done."

"Right now I don't think anybody but me could make head or tail out of them. But I'll probably be calling for help later, when we set up tables and so on."

"Be sure you do now."

"Edna Barker's never brought anything but scalloped potatoes for fifteen years." Zelda sighed again. "I suppose there's no use trying to suggest anything else to her—very indifferent scalloped potatoes, too—''

The kitchen suddenly came alive with noise as someone knocked on the back door and at the same moment the telephone in the front hall rang. Zelda pushed back her chair. "I'll get the phone. It's probably someone on the committee. You see who's at the door, will you, dear?"

Hannah got up and opened the door to see Jake standing there, and felt at once that swift turnover of her heart. He was dressed for work in his usual jeans and plaid shirt, sleeves rolled up over muscular forearms. He glanced behind her at the empty kitchen and pulled her to him, giving her a long hard kiss before saying a word. Then slowly he released her and stepped back. He ran his tongue around his lips and said, "Blueberry?"

She gave a low giggle. "Banana. Want one?"

He followed her inside. "Actually, no. I can't stay."

From the front hall they could hear Zelda's exasperated voice. "Really, Melanie, there's a limit to how much coleslaw we can use...."

"I love you," he murmured, pulling her close.

She allowed herself to be enfolded in his arms, to feel strength and love surrounding her, engulfing her, until she could scarcely breathe. "Jake..." She could only whisper his name.

"Want to spend the day with me?" he asked, finally loosening his hold.

She nodded. "Going on calls?"

"Something different today. I'm having a rabies clinic at the school. Do it every year. Usually Carrie comes along to help, but she won't be back from her trip till late in the day. Would you fill in for her?"

"Just looking for cheap help?" She smiled, circling his waist with her arms and looking up at him.

"That's one of the side benefits," he said, grinning back. "But mostly I can't stand the idea of not seeing you until tonight."

"Okay. I'll come."

They pulled away from each other reluctantly as they heard Zelda hang up. When she returned to the kitchen she was shaking her head in mild despair. "Hello, Jake," she said when she saw him. "Every year I say I won't work on this thing again, and every year I get hooked."

"Just don't invite Assemblyman Taggart to be the guest speaker," he advised. "Last year he put half the audience to sleep by the time he was finished."

"Don't worry, I won't," Zelda promised. "How about Reverend Watson? He ought to be okay. And of course Peyton Harrison will make the opening remarks. Grandson of the founder," she explained to Hannah. "We can't very well leave him out." She pushed up her sliding glasses and turned suddenly to Jake. "Isn't this your clinic day at the school gym?"

"It is. I've just enlisted a helper to take over for Carrie."

Zelda's glance went from one to the other, a knowing but affectionate look. "Well, that's good," she said. "I think she ought to do just fine."

JAKE AND HANNAH arrived at the school to find Tully already there ahead of them unloading the cartons of vaccine and disposable needles. A few early customers were also on hand, children and adults with apprehensive dogs on leashes, and there was a moderate amount of yipping and barking as they waited.

"Be with you shortly," Jake called to them as he and Hannah went around the building to the school yard, where a large table and two smaller ones had been set up under a broad-spreading copper beech tree. Tully was unpacking syringes and Jake began filling them with vaccine and laying them out on one of the small tables.

"Here's your stuff," he said to Hannah. He handed her a pile of certificates and a box of metal tags. "Fill out a certificate for each dog or cat. Owner's name here, pet's name, date. Then give them a tag to go on the collar and collect a dollar from them."

"Only a dollar?" she asked, surprised. "That doesn't seem like very much."

"That's what I tell him," Tully chimed in. "That don't more'n cover the cost of the vaccine and the needles."

"It's important that they come, that's the main thing," Jake said.

"Will there be many?"

"We ought to be busy most of the day." He smiled. "Think you're up to it?"

"You bet. Bring 'em on." She watched as he returned to the big table, her eyes following the easy stride, the sun-browned arms, the hair that always seemed to fall forward when he concentrated on something.

"Okay, Tully, bring 'em on," he ordered, echoing Hannah's words with a grin.

Hannah was amazed at the number of pets that appeared during the course of the day. Tully explained to her that they came not just from Harrison Falls, but from all over the county—Dr. Jake McCabe's clinics were well-known. There were both cats and dogs, some shivering apprehensively, some displaying aloof unconcern until the actual moment of inoculation. Hannah sat at one of the small tables and filled in certificates, handed out tags and collected money. Always out of the corner of her eye she was aware of Jake and what he was doing. While Tully held each cat or dog, Jake would pat it reassuringly; if the animal was brought by a child, he always had a few words of praise for it, making the lowliest mongrel sound like a champion. Most of the owners he greeted by name, and even some of the pets. Every now and then his glance would move toward Hannah, and when it did, their eyes would lock in silent communication and she would see a smile playing at the corners of his mouth.

The words that had come to her when she sat at her window in the moments just before dawn that morning recurred to Hannah over and over. *Have I ever been this happy?*

He brought her back to Zelda's at the end of the long afternoon. "Take a little rest," he said. "You must be worn out. You were a big help to me."

"I'm not a bit tired," she insisted. "I enjoyed it."

"Even so, it was a long day. Only not quite long enough—not yet." He brought his mouth down to hers suddenly, and her arms slid up to circle his neck. For a moment he pressed her close to him, then whispered in her ear, "I'll be back for you later."

She watched him take the steps two at a time, climb into the Jeep and drive off down the lane, one arm waving at her as he went.

Despite her protests of not being tired, the hot bath she took in Zelda's old-fashioned tub felt as delicious as the bath she'd taken on the day of her arrival in Harrison Falls. And as on that day, she stretched out on the bed afterward, with the "bear paw" quilt covering her, and fell asleep instantly. When she awoke and padded downstairs, barefoot and wearing her terry-cloth robe, Zelda was just coming into the front hall.

"Oh, there you are. I have a message for you. From Jake."

Hannah's heart gave the bounce that was becoming familiar to her at the mention of his name.

"I told him you were sleeping because I'd peeked in at you before, and he said I wasn't to wake you, just tell you he's been called out on a calf case and you'd better not wait up for him."

"Oh. All right." Her disappointment was tempered by the fact that he had called, had told Zelda not to wake her, had been thinking about her.

"How long does a case like that take usually?"

"To pull a calf? Oh, hard to say. Could be hours. And it was quite a distance he went—farm over on the other side of the interstate. I know the people—Judson, their name is." Zelda was giving her a curious look, not asking any questions, but Hannah was sure she was reading the situation with unerring accuracy. "Come on now, let's have a bite of supper and I'll tell you all about the Founder's Day committee meeting this afternoon. I'm sure you're dying to hear that," she added with a grin.

"Okay." Hannah smiled back. "Let me slip some clothes on. Be right with you."

As she pulled on her jeans and T-shirt Hannah glanced out through the open window of her room, across Zelda's yard, out to where low rolling hills began far in the distance. Something nagged and nibbled at the back of her mind. Some puzzle, something left unsolved, something she'd been planning to pursue before the wonder of Jake's love had crashed into her life, scattering all other thoughts.

Suddenly she remembered.

"Have you got a county map around here some-where?" she asked Zelda as she slid into her place at the kitchen table.

"Sure. In one of these drawers, I think." Zelda put a bowl of salad on the table, then began flinging open drawers in the old wooden cabinets. They squeaked and stuck stubbornly, but Zelda persisted, tossing out balls of string, can openers, pot holders, nutcrackers, boxes of cough drops, and finally coming up triumphantly with a worn, much folded map.

"There. I knew it was here somewhere." She handed it to Hannah. "Thinking of doing some exploring?"

"Yes, that's just what I was thinking," Hannah said, relieved Zelda had put it that way so that she wouldn't feel obligated to lie about it. For some reason she was reluctant to admit the exact nature of what she planned to do. "There's still a couple of hours of daylight left and it would be a good chance for me to drive around a little."

"Well, I'd be happy to go along and show you things," Zelda said, "only Dottie Barnes and I are going down to the church to count chairs and tables—see how many we're going to need."

"Oh, that's all right. Another time," Hannah said, throwing a smile over her shoulder as she hurried out the door.

She had a general idea of the direction to take, for twice now she'd been to the Harrisons' hilltop estate and so was familiar with the winding road that led there. But that was the wrong route for tonight's exploration. Just past the village she pulled over onto the shoulder and spread Zelda's worn county map out on the steering wheel of the Porsche. She picked out the main roads, traced the bold blue slash of the interstate, then began concentrating on the thin black lines that led into less traveled areas. She found the Harrisons' road, called Harrison Drive, naturally enough, and figured out which route the hunt club had taken on the day of the working party. For several minutes she studied the lay of the land, then folded the map along its limp creases and resumed her journey. She drove slowly now, watching for road signs and arrows, and at last made a right turn onto a narrow paved road. After three miles, it changed to hard-packed dirt. There were few houses along the way—one or two ramshackle trailers and some abandoned barns that looked ready to cave in. Weeds and brush crowded the edges of the road. Then the road began to climb gradually, growing steeper as she drove. She took care over ruts and bumps, but twice the sleek low car scraped ominously over something in the roadway. After a quarter of an hour the way leveled out again. She was on top of a hill now, and ahead of her the land stretched out flat and open and barren. With a sharp intake of breath, Hannah realized she was back at the strange tract she'd discovered that day on her solitary horseback ride.

Prompted by some instinct she couldn't explain, Hannah drove the car onto a narrow track to the right, away from the road. Then she opened the door and got out, putting on dark glasses against the long slanting rays of the late sun.

It was just as she remembered—scarred and desolate, marked by heavy tire tracks. Yet she had the feeling it wasn't entirely the same. Something had been changed, or perhaps added. Something was there that hadn't been there the week before. She squinted and shaded her eyes, studying it more carefully, and now she could see an object half-buried in the rubbly earth but sticking out, a barrel or metal drum, perhaps.

A feeling rose in Hannah, a response that was so familiar it felt like an old friend. It was something she hadn't felt since leaving New York, in spite of all the sketches and descriptions she'd sent to Bob Anderson. She was in the presence of a story. An instinct deep in her bones told her so. For several minutes she stood there looking, almost as if waiting for the reality of it to take shape before her. And suddenly it did, looming on the horizon opposite her—a huge dump truck rumbling up from the opposite direction.

Instinctively Hannah dodged behind a clump of brush on the edge of the cleared land, watching as the truck made its purposeful way to the area where the half-buried drum lay. It halted there, and she could hear the grinding of gears as the truck bed was lifted to discharge its load. More drums came tumbling out along with a quantity of other material Hannah couldn't identify. She crept cautiously from behind the brush and tried to make out the lettering painted on the side of the truck, but she was too far away. Then as she watched, another truck lumbered up in the track of the first and brought its load to the same spot. She could see the figures of the two men, one in the cab of the second truck, along with the driver of the first one who'd jumped out onto the ground and was now engaged in conversation with him.

Hannah crept closer, trying to see better, and was finally able to make out the lettering on the lead truck: Acme Disposal, General Trucking. Hannah suddenly realized that, away from the protection of the undergrowth, she'd be in plain sight if the men should turn in her direction. She began edging slowly back and was just slipping behind the clump of brush when the man on the ground did turn her way. Hannah's breath caught in her throat and she held it, not daring to breathe while he seemed to scan the landscape before turning back and resuming his conversation.

The light was changing as the sun sank lower. Crouching behind the bush, Hannah was beginning to feel cramped by the time the two trucks started up. For a moment she feared they would head toward her and make their exit by the narrow road she had taken, but instead they circled and returned the way they had come. When they had disappeared from sight she went back to her car and for several minutes sat there behind the wheel as the light faded around her, turning to a blue twilight.

Now her thoughts came tumbling out, one after the other, in a ferment of speculation. She had seen the name on the lead truck, Acme Disposal, but that told her little. The trucks had been hired by some factory or plant. And what industry was there in this town except—Hannah paused, frowned and tried to put it all together. They had taken a back road and arrived just before dark, so apparently they didn't want to be seen. Which meant that it must be more than just an ordinary landfill operation. It was—Hannah was sure of it— a toxic waste dump. Materials were being dumped here illegally. Then who had hired the truckers? The only factory in the area was Harrison Electrical, and as far as she could determine, the waste was being disposed of on Harrison land.

Slowly Hannah started the car and pulled back onto the narrow dirt road. She must get home and wait for Jake to return. She must talk it over with him, report what she'd seen, plan with him what their next move should be. She drove a little faster once she reached the highway, watching the night-flying insects caught in the glare when she turned on the headlights. But the farther she drove, the closer she got to the village, the more doubts began to creep into her thinking.

This was a big story. It could have ramifications far beyond the narrow confines of Harrison Falls. It was the kind of matter that could stir up animosities, resentments, pull the town apart. Jake had grown up here. She was, after all, the outsider, the city girl, the stranger in their midst. What would happen to the peaceful atmosphere, the congenial friendliness of the inhabitants if she were to explode this story like a grenade among them? What right had she to set neighbor against neighbor, placing them at odds, perhaps tearing the fabric of the community? She was fairly sure there was no love lost between Jake and Walker. If she knew this, surely others did, too. And if Jake was involved in the accusation—if *she* involved him—the town might very well consider it no more than evidence of an old grudge. Wouldn't it be wiser to handle it herself, quietly, even if it meant leaving Jake outside the matter? Hannah caught her breath nervously as she thought about it.

She approached the outskirts of the village, but instead of heading toward home she took a turn down the road that led to the lake. Jake had shown it to her, and she and Zelda had come that way once. When she reached the lakeshore, quiet and serene in the near darkness, Hannah stopped the car and parked, sitting perfectly still for a long time. At last she opened the door and got out, standing by the car and looking over the water, feeling the evening breeze riffle her hair, watching a nearly full moon rising low on the horizon.

She loved Jake McCabe. And she believed that he loved her. Facing it squarely, admitting it to herself, she knew this was the most important thing that had ever happened to her. Did she dare take a chance that she might lose that love now? She had covered enough major news stories to know she could handle this one, but what she would have to do must alienate Jake beyond any reconciliation. Could she bear to do it? And what was the alternative? If the whole town were thrown into quarreling and chaos over her discovery, might Jake not begin to resent her, no matter how correct her surmises?

Hannah watched the silvery streak of the moon's reflection in the softly moving water, listened to the gentle lapping of waves on the pebbly shore. Once or twice she swallowed hard, and finally the tears she could no longer hold back welled up and coursed down her cheeks. She knew what she had to do—but would their love be strong enough to survive it?

CHAPTER NINE

"WHY DON'T YOU come with me?" Jake asked. "It'll only be three days, but how can I stand to be away from you that long?"

Jake's arm slid around Hannah's shoulders. They sat close together on Zelda's porch swing in the warm summer evening while from inside came the sound of Zelda and Carrie in earnest discussion. "Those hives over on Mr. Stimson's farm are going to need two more supers at least," Carrie was saying. "The bees filled the ones we put in last month."

"Already?" they could hear Zelda answer. "You're going to have a bigger harvest than last year, I do believe."

Hannah smiled over at Jake. "Where are you going?" she asked.

"All the way to the other side of the county where the big dairy herds are. I have to stop at several farms and it's easier to stay there while I vaccinate all the calves for brucellosis. Should be home late Wednesday night."

"Now, you know I couldn't possibly go with you," Hannah said with a mock-serious look. "Everyone over there would be scandalized, not to mention everyone here in Harrison Falls. This isn't New York City, you know. Besides, Zelda and I will be working all week on the Founder's Day picnic plans. I can't tell you how many committees she's put me on—officially or not."

He sighed. "Well, I'll just have to take Tully along then. Although he's nowhere near as pretty as you." He pulled her close to him and bent to plant a long, lingering kiss on her mouth. "I'll be thinking about you every minute," he whispered.

Hannah turned to put her arms around his neck, and she kissed him back, urgently, and as if it was for the last time. *But it isn't,* she insisted to herself. *It can't be.* Yet even as she told herself that, a nagging doubt persisted, a dark threatening presence lying far back in her mind.

ON MONDAY Carrie appeared at Zelda's, carrying her nightgown and toothbrush in a paper bag. "I always stay with Zelda when Dad has to be away at night," she explained to Hannah.

"Well, we'll keep you busy this week," Zelda promised. "First I'll run you over to Stimson's farm with those extra supers for your hives. Then you can help me with some telephoning."

"Okay," Carrie agreed, and Hannah, listening to them make plans, decided it would be a good day to start the business she had in mind. "I've written the publicity piece for the local paper," she told Zelda, "and I've taken care of getting those posters up. Is there anything else you need me for today? I have a few things to do, if it's okay," she added casually, and Zelda waved her off, pushing her glasses into position and consulting a dog-eared list. "Was it Mrs. Esmond who brought that wonderful strawberry-rhubarb pie last year?" She frowned, looking toward the ceiling. "I believe I'll ask if she'll bring two this year."

Once Zelda and Carrie had left in the pickup, Hannah quickly got into her own car and headed for the village. At the drugstore she stopped to pick up film for her camera.

"Do you send your film out of town to be developed?" she inquired of the girl behind the counter.

"Oh, yes, but our service is fast. Twenty-four hours or two days at the most."

Hannah nodded and smiled as she left. She preferred to have the pictures developed somewhere other than Harrison Falls. She got back in the car and retraced the route she had taken the night she'd driven to the dump site. Bumping along the back roads, she found her pulse pounding with nervous excitement, yet her brain, the part that was figuring out every move, was functioning coolly and logically. Thoughts of Jake kept crowding in, but when they did, she pushed them firmly away. That could all be sorted out later, she told herself, and a small voice in her head retorted, *If there is a later*. But Hannah refused to listen to it and instead thought ahead to what she had to do next.

Now, in broad daylight, the dump was deserted and, except for the noxious-looking metal drums, appeared quite innocent. Hannah didn't trouble to hide her car this time and walked across the rutted area with her camera to get close-ups of the place where she'd seen the two trucks. There was a heavy, sweetish odor hanging over the area that made her wrinkle her nose in distaste. When she had shot half of her film she returned to her car and drove back the way she'd come.

But she didn't go straight home. Instead, she watched for turnings, finding that she was becoming increasingly familiar with the roads, and made her way to the Rittenmyers' farm, where Carrie had coaxed the swarm of bees into the hive and where she and Jake had discovered the calf that day—it seemed a lifetime ago. This was the place, she recalled with a twisting pang, where he had held her and kissed her beside the little stream. Pushing that memory far back in her mind, she drove up to the white farmhouse, prepared with an excuse if someone should be there to greet her: Zelda had sent her to ask Mrs. Rittenmyer if she would bring her three-bean salad to the picnic Saturday, she would say. However, no one was home, so Hannah jumped out of the car and hurried toward the hilly field and the little stream where the cow had hidden her calf. She climbed purposefully up the slope, taking pictures as she went, and when she reached the top, traced the course of the stream with her eye as far as she could see it. Unquestionably it led upward in the direction of the high flat area where the waste dump was. She hurried back down the hill and turned her car in the direction of town, this time going directly to the drugstore and leaving her film to be developed.

While she was in the drugstore she spotted a public telephone booth and after a search through the phone book, dialed a number in the state capital and spoke at length. Only then did she get back in her car and head for home.

THAT EVENING as she sat in her room working on some notes, there was a soft knock on the bedroom door, which she'd left ajar. Carrie stuck her head in.

"Come on in, Carrie," Hannah said, putting down her notebook and pen.

Carrie, in a long pink nightgown, stepped inside. She was carrying the puppy in her arms.

"He came to my room," she said.

"I didn't even know he was missing! Goodness, he's going to be ready for a leash next. What do you think?"

Carrie plopped into a chair, still holding Sam. "It wouldn't hurt to try," she said doubtfully. "It must be time for him to have his shots, too."

"Oh, goodness, already?" Hannah had a moment's fleeting vision of Jake in his white coat, leaning over Sam, his hair falling forward the way it always did when he was concentrating on something. She pushed the image quickly away.

Carrie took the sleeping puppy and placed him carefully in his basket, then wandered to the dressing table and sat down in front of it, looking with interest at the foundations, blushers, eye shadows. Hannah, following her glance, reflected with amusement that she'd used hardly any of them since her first day here. A quick touch of lipstick was all she bothered with these days.

"Could I try some of these?" Carrie asked.

"Yes, if you promise to wash it off afterward."

Carrie's eyes lit up as she selected eye shadow and began applying it. Hannah smiled, watching her. "I hear your mother's invited you to California for a visit this summer," she said.

"Yes, but I'm not going." Carrie's tongue came out and touched her upper lip as she concentrated on the task at hand.

"Oh? Why not? Wouldn't you like to?"

"Well...it's not that I don't want to," Carrie said. "But see, she's getting married this summer. I never even met this guy. I'd just be in the way."

"I'm sure that's not how your mom feels at all. She'd probably like very much for you to meet him. It must be a wonderful and exciting time for her, and she wants you to share it with her."

CITY GIRL, COUNTRY GIRL

Carrie put down the eye shadow and examined the array of tubes and bottles. "Does this come next?" she asked, picking up an eyeliner pencil.

"Yes, but not too much," Hannah cautioned. Then she went on, "You're growing older, you know, and maybe your mother feels she'd like to know you better—find out what kind of person you are. After all, if she hadn't wanted you to be there for her wedding, wouldn't she just have written you about it, or telephoned? It seems to me you're quite lucky, when you stop to think about it. To have your home here and all the things you love, and to have a nice place to visit, as well."

Carrie finished the wavering lines around her eyes and picked up a brush to apply blusher. She hesitated, holding it in midair, and it seemed to Hannah that she was turning the matter over in her mind. "Well," she began seriously, "maybe I might just *think* about it. I still don't know if I want to go, but if I do decide to..." She hesitated, then the words came out all in a rush. "Would you maybe help me pick out a dress to wear to the wedding? A really nice one?"

"Of course I would. I'd love to."

Carrie went on applying makeup and at last stopped and regarded herself in the mirror. Her blue eyes were dark-rimmed and the blusher was somewhat higher on one cheek than the other. She sighed and said, "Well, I guess I have to wash it off. May I use your bathroom, Hannah?"

"Help yourself."

When she returned after several minutes of splashing, she looked once more her young blooming self, angelic in the long pink gown. She headed for the door, then paused and turned back. "You know, Hannah, my dad really likes you a whole lot."

Hannah could feel her face flooding with color. "Well, I like him, too," she said, trying to keep her voice steady. "I like both of you. A whole lot."

"Do you have to go back to New York City?"

"Yes, eventually. It's where my work is. Where I live."

"It would be nice if you could stay here," Carrie said wistfully.

"Well, unfortunately we can't always do the things we want," Hannah said, trying to keep a bitter tone out of her voice.

THE WAITING ROOM was jammed with patients, Hannah saw, as she entered with Sam. Dogs and cats, in and out of carrying cases, on leashes, in the arms of their owners. Some of the animals were trembling with apprehension, some whining and shivering, some sleeping nonchalantly. She knew Jake was back; she'd heard his Jeep roaring out of the driveway early that morning. Now, seeing the crowd waiting for him, it dawned on her that being away for three days had probably set him back considerably in his practice here. She was about to turn around and leave—Sam's shots could, after all, wait for a less busy time—when the door to the examining room opened and Jake appeared, his eyes scanning the crowd and coming to rest on her almost at once. She saw his concentration dissolve and a soft look of pleasure replace it. His eyes sparkled at her. "Fine, Miss Chase, I'm glad you were able to come immediately," he said. "Mrs. Maxwell, please take Holly into the next room. I'll be with you directly. Tully's in there. He'll help you lift her onto the table." He stood aside for Hannah to enter, then closed the door behind her, and, all in one motion, spun around and took her in his arms. "Hannah—you don't know how much I missed you...."

His mouth sought hers in an enveloping kiss that ended only when small squeals were heard from Sam, caught in the embrace along with Hannah. They parted, laughing, and Hannah said, "Your other patients will be cross. You shouldn't have taken me ahead of them."

"That's why I made it sound like an emergency—which it was. I couldn't have lasted much longer without seeing you. I got in around midnight last night and I've been on the go since six this morning. Had to go pull a calf then, and it hasn't let up since. I figure if I work like blazes the rest of the week I'll be able to get free for the picnic on Saturday."

Hannah swallowed uneasily and turned to place Sam on the examining table. "The way Zelda's put me to work, you'd better not count on us going together. I'll see you there—how will that be? She's got a million things lined up for me to do."

"Oh? Well, okay, I guess." He glanced at her, then gave a tolerant laugh and said, "Sure, that'll be all right."

Just for an instant, though, she had seen hesitation and a question in his eyes. "How do you like the new collar and leash?" she asked quickly. Sam, on the table, was hunkering down and trying to back out of the collar. The red leash was in a tangle around his feet.

"Haven't been able to look at anything but you," he said softly and leaned over to kiss her again, a long slow kiss that made Hannah go limp with desire. She had to force herself to pull away.

"We're here for shots, you know, Doctor," she said with pretended primness. "Carrie said it was time."

He sighed and turned to prepare a syringe. "Can you keep from fainting when I jab him?"

"I'll make an effort," she said teasingly. "Even though I'm just a sentimental woman."

He gave her back a rueful smile. "My words return to haunt me," he groaned.

"It won't hurt him really, will it?" she asked then.

"I doubt he'll even realize what's happening."

If only she herself could get through the next few days that easily, Hannah thought with a sinking heart.

She tried to walk Sam on the new red leash as they wandered home along the path, but he kept pulling backward and whimpering, and at last she scooped him up and carried him. Try as she might, she couldn't keep the tears from welling up in her eyes and spilling down her cheeks. Sam lifted his head and began licking her face enthusiastically, and Hannah hugged him tight. *I can't go through with it, I can't,* she repeated over and over. But what she had in her handbag was burning against her like fire. The pictures she had just picked up at the drugstore. How could she not go through with it, with what she knew now?

Resolutely, before she could change her mind, she went to the telephone as soon as she arrived home. "Walker? It's Hannah Chase."

"Hannah! What a wonderful surprise! Where have you been keeping yourself?"

"Oh, right here. Only I've been very busy. Are you going to be at the picnic on Saturday?"

"Wouldn't miss it."

"I thought maybe we might go together."

His voice sounded delighted. "What a great idea! Nothing I'd like better. What time?"

"Well, I remember your saying you usually do some work at the plant on Saturday mornings. Why don't I pick you up there?"

"You wouldn't mind? That would be terrific."

"Okay. Will you be done by noon?"

"Even earlier. How about eleven?"

"Eleven it is."

Hannah replaced the instrument quietly, and the tears she had shed earlier were dry now, replaced by a steely cold determination.

No matter how hard it had been, she felt she'd done what she had to. She was convinced she was right about the matter of the toxic dump, but hunches had been wrong before. And suppose she *had* made a mistake. Jake shouldn't be involved in any of it. The whole town knew he and Walker were not on the best of terms—she recalled the angry scene between the two of them in the stable at the Harrisons' party that day. If she confided in him and he became part of it and it all came to nothing, the townspeople would think he'd been vindictive and petty and out to settle a grudge against Walker. Such quarrels could create animosities and bad feeling that would last for years. This wasn't her town, it was Jake's. She had to do it this way because she loved him. It was as simple as that.

Well, there was no turning back now. Right or wrong, she'd made her decision. But her heart throbbed with pain and seemed to say Jake's name with every beat. Would she ever be given a chance to explain?

SHE DRESSED in white pants, a turquoise knit top and sneakers when she got up on Saturday morning. Sunglasses rested on top of her head and a white sweater was carelessly knotted around her neck. She and Carrie, who'd arrived at the house early, had helped Zelda load the pickup with pies, cakes, a handmade quilt to be raffled, extra paper plates and cups and two gallon jugs of iced tea. Then the two of them had left, heading for the park, with Hannah promising to follow in her own car.

The day had turned out be be perfect, as Zelda had predicted—a few fluffy clouds in a sky of clear bright blue. But Hannah scarcely noticed as she hurried back into the house to get ready. It was too early to pick up Walker, but she was going to leave the house, anyway— the sooner the better, in case Jake should take it into his head to stop by and see if she was free to ride with him, after all. She left Sam in his penned-in kitchen area with plenty of food and water, making a mental note to check on him after a few hours, and dashed into the front hall where she'd left her camera. She stopped long enough to rip open a fresh package of film and was just starting to load the camera, fingers fumbling and trembling unaccountably, when she heard a car in the driveway, and a moment later, a loud knock on the door.

Hannah's heart leapt into her throat, and she froze with the camera in her hand. Her car was parked in the driveway, but mightn't he think she'd gone on ahead with Zelda in the pickup? For a moment she held her breath in panic, and then, trying to be sensible and rational, she hesitantly opened the door.

"Oh, great, you're still here," Jake said, smiling broadly. He was dressed for the picnic in jeans and a spotless white shirt, sleeves rolled up as always. "Look, I even washed it." He waved in the direction of the gleaming Jeep, parked behind him on the drive. "I know you said you'd probably be all tied up helping Zelda, but I thought I'd take a chance, anyway. Are you ready?"

For a moment Hannah stood quite still in the doorway, looking at him, at his broad happy smile, his tousled hair, at the slim, muscular body that she now knew well. *Couldn't I do it all differently?* she asked herself in sudden desperation. *How can I bear to hurt him this way?*

"I haven't seen you all week," he said softly. "We have a lot to make up for."

Hannah squared her shoulders and took a deep breath. "Jake, I'm terribly sorry—I should have told you. I promised to go to the picnic with Walker Harrison."

He looked as if she'd struck him. The depth of pain in his eyes astonished and dismayed her.

"I see," he said curtly.

Hannah felt a desperate need to explain, at least partially. "Jake, there are things you don't know about Walker—"

He cut her off. "And it looks like there's a lot I don't know about you," he said, turning and taking the porch steps in a single stride, flinging himself into the Jeep and roaring off down the lane.

For several minutes Hannah stood in the doorway gazing after him, and all that kept pounding in her head were the words of an old song she had once heard: "There goes my heart..." At last she closed the door and turned back almost absentmindedly to the business of loading her camera. Her hands had stopped trembling, but they were icy cold now, and tears kept getting in the way of what she was doing.

SHE HAD TO TRAVEL a stretch of used-car lots, fast-food outlets and gas stations to reach the Harrison Electrical plant, but when she arrived there she found it tastefully landscaped and set well back from the road. Now, on Saturday, there were only a few cars in the employee parking lot. She saw Walker's little sports car and parked near it. For a moment she sat quite still in her own car, leaning forward with her head on the steering wheel, willing herself into a state of concentration on the matter at hand. Whatever happened between Jake and her, this business was important. And more than two people were involved; it concerned a whole town. She had started it, come this far. She would see it through. Bob Anderson would be proud of that kind of resolution, she thought wryly. She wondered whether it would be enough compensation to see her through the lonely life she saw ahead of her.

She took a deep breath and raised her head, planning her next move. If she could get inside, ask for a brief tour of the plant, it was possible something would reveal itself to her, something she could follow up on. As of now, she had only circumstantial evidence, but if she asked the right questions, some small piece of information might point to an avenue she could pursue. She started to open the car door, then suddenly gasped. On the far side of the building, almost beyond her line of vision, a truck was rolling up and stopping. She couldn't quite make out the lettering, but she was almost sure it was the name she'd seen at the dump site. Acme Disposal.

Alert and concentrating now, Hannah grabbed her camera and slid out of the car, hurrying across the lot to the main building. She kept close to it and ran, half crouching, to the corner where the truck was parked. As she approached it, she slowed her pace and ducked behind some shrubbery, which had been planted there in a cluster. Sinking into softly turned earth and peat moss, she held her breath and took out her camera, adjusted the zoom lens and leaned forward as far as she dared. She could hear two male voices.

"...told you it wasn't a good idea for you to come here by daylight." Hannah was sure it was Walker Harrison's voice.

"Well, hell, it's Saturday. You always said Saturday morning was okay."

"I know, but I'm expecting someone."

"So they'll see a truck. Big deal."

"All right, all right. What's this problem you spoke about?"

"Well, I been worried, that's all. The whole thing's getting risky."

"I suppose you're building up to asking for more money." Walker's voice curled with sarcasm.

"No, I ain't. What we got to do is find a new site. People are getting nosy about this one. I thought I saw someone up there the other night."

Hannah focused her camera and began shooting quickly, hoping the shutter's click would be inaudible to the two men.

"That place is on our own property—what kind of trouble could there be? I can handle things. Don't worry..."

They shifted away from her and their voices faded. Hannah saw something change hands—money, she was sure—and then the trucker turned and swung up into his cab. Hannah backed out of the thick shrubbery and retraced her steps, stopping once to brush the soft mulch off her sneakers. She returned to her car and tossed the camera onto the front seat. Then she slipped her sunglasses on, smoothed her hair, picking a twig out of it, and strolled casually up to the front door.

Inside the lobby of the building, it was dim and cool. Far down at the other end of the corridor, Walker Harrison was already coming toward her.

"Hi, there," he called out. "I was just on my way to look for you—didn't see you drive up."

Hoping with all her heart that this was true, Hannah said cheerfully, "Just got here. Are you ready?" She no longer needed to ask for a tour of the factory; whatever she needed was stored in her camera, and now she was anxious to be out of here as quickly as possible.

"Ready and eager." He laughed, grabbing her arm and planting a kiss on her cheek. "This was a wonderful idea. Today's going to be fun. You know, Dad's been up since daylight practicing his speech. I keep telling him it's only opening remarks they want from him, but I think he's prepared to hold forth for an hour."

Hannah managed a laugh as they hurried across the parking lot and got into her car. He picked up her camera and looked it over with interest as she reversed and headed back toward the road.

"This looks very professional," he said. "Planning on capturing the town in informal poses today?"

"Oh, you know—once a reporter, always a reporter," she said lightly, turning left on the state highway toward the village.

CHAPTER TEN

THE FOUNDER'S DAY picnic was in full swing by the time Hannah and Walker arrived and found a parking space on a side street. Making their way toward the green municipal park with its center statue of a Civil War soldier, they could see the massed balloons, gaily decorated booths and long trestle tables covered with food. At one side a small platform had been set up, and wooden chairs were arranged in rows before it. Children were dashing between the legs of grown-ups, sometimes accompanied by dogs, throwing themselves on the grass, laughing and shouting. Behind the food tables Hannah could see Zelda in a summery print dress with an apron over it. She was busily pointing and nodding, overseeing the distribution of casseroles and platters. A young man with a sound system was fiddling with tapes and knobs before slipping in a cassette. Music burst forth, too loudly, and was quickly toned down. As Hannah and Walker approached the park, a long low convertible drove up. Leslie Harte was driving, her daughter Bethany in the front seat with her, and her father, dignified in a white suit, sitting in the back.

Hannah's breath caught painfully as she saw Jake step forward to open the car door.

"Oh, dear, I don't believe they'll let me park here, will they?" Leslie said worriedly.

"Never mind. You folks get out and I'll find a place for the car," Jake reassured her. "I think they'll soon be ready for you, Mr. Harrison. Hello, Bethany. Carrie was just asking if you'd come. Leslie, give me your keys. I'll take care of the parking."

Hannah watched Leslie slide out, elegant-looking in a long tunic of bright pink silk over white silk pants. She wore dainty sandals and her blond hair was tied back with a soft silk scarf that matched the tunic. Hannah longed to turn around and approach by another route, but Walker was smiling and propelling her toward the group.

"Hey, Bethany—hi!" It was Carrie, coming on the run. "Come and give me a hand, will you? I'm slicing lemons for Zelda, and after that I think she's going to hit me with making more sandwiches. She says there's never enough."

"Okay, sure," Bethany said, and the two ran off together, legs pumping and hair flying.

"Well!" Leslie's blue eyes widened with disbelief. "I certainly can't get her to do *that* at home!" Carrie's voice drifted back. "Hey, you know what, Bethany? I might go to California this summer." A look of surprise crossed Jake's face and for the briefest instant his eyes sought Hannah's as she and Walker joined them. Then he looked away quickly and Leslie exclaimed, "Hannah! How lovely to see you. Isn't this just the most fun? I didn't even know till this morning that you and Walker were coming together."

Jake's voice cut in clearly, "Oh, yes, Hannah's full of surprises."

Hannah gave him a quick glance and saw his sardonic smile. She felt a coldness around her heart and clasped her hands tightly together, trying to conceal her sudden misery. Peyton Harrison chimed in with, "Wonderful day, wonderful. Nothing like the Founder's Day picnic. And always good weather for it, you notice?"

Hannah made an effort to sound casual. "Yes, I certainly don't want to miss anything."

"Or anyone," Jake said. "Will this be your last big fling before returning to New York, Hannah?" His eyebrows arched at her.

Before she could answer, Walker was saying, "Hey, none of that talk. We want Hannah to stay with us, don't we? She's made it a great summer for all of us."

"Yes, of course," Leslie put in warmly. She pressed against Jake, holding his arm and dropping the car keys into his palm. "There, darling, if you insist—it's sweet of you to help." She gave Hannah a sidelong look. "And I'm sure we'll talk Hannah out of rushing back to New York, won't we, Jake?"

The air felt icicle-sharp and cold to Hannah in spite of the warm summer sun overhead. "Oh, I doubt if that would do any good," Jake said, his mouth quirking up at one corner. "Hannah does what she wants, I'm afraid." He slipped an arm around Leslie's slim waist. "Why don't you and your dad go over to the platform and see where they want him to sit? Then I'll join you and we'll get seats for the program."

"See you all later," Walker said easily. "Hannah, you and I'd better make the rounds and see everything, don't you think?"

"Yes, of course." Hannah moved away with him, but the icy cold moved with her and the day stretched ahead of her, agonizing and endless.

Hours passed in a blur as Hannah wandered from booth to booth, looking away quickly from the concern in Zelda's eyes, smiling automatically and shaking hands when Walker made introductions. She was aware of the noise and laughter around her, aware of the sunlight and dappled shade, the music and voices, but all of it seemed strangely remote to her. Over and over her eyes kept returning to Jake as he moved through the crowd with Leslie at his side. Hannah saw him bending to say something to her, saw them laughing together, saw Leslie's head rest on his shoulder. When the crowd grew quiet and settled down for the speeches, she saw the two sitting close together, saw Leslie's hand creep into Jake's and stay there.

And when the afternoon had at last worn itself out and small children were beginning to fall asleep in their mothers' arms, it was Leslie who put the official end to the day.

"Really, we must be going," she said, coming up to where Hannah and Walker were standing near the statue in the center of the square. She looked as fresh as when she'd arrived, blond hair sleek, makeup perfect. "Hannah, if you're really thinking of leaving us soon, and if I don't see you again, all the best of luck." Her small hand came out in farewell, and Hannah took it reluctantly. For a moment their eyes met, and Hannah could see in Leslie's a gleam of triumph, a satisfaction the other woman couldn't quite hide. "If you ever come back to Harrison Falls, things may look quite different to you."

"Oh, really?" Hannah managed a small smile.

"Yes, I think I've finally talked Jake into that piece of property I told you about. We may be getting the construction under way before you know it."

Hannah nodded politely, noticing she had said *we*. "All the best of luck to you, too, Leslie," she murmured. She kept her eyes firmly fixed on Leslie's triumphant smile, not daring to let her glance stray to Jake, who stood at Leslie's side, but her cheeks burned feverishly and she could feel the piercing accusation in his look even without seeing it.

"How about dinner now? Some nice quiet place where we can relax?" Walker said brightly when the others had left them.

Hannah hesitated. "Oh, I don't know," she began. "I'm really awfully tired—I mean, it was quite a long day—"

"All the more reason to unwind and take it easy. Besides, you hardly ate a thing all afternoon."

"I wasn't really hungry, I guess." But Hannah could feel the feebleness of her protests and thought with dismay that the day still wasn't over.

IT WAS TEN O'CLOCK before she managed to convince Walker that she really was spent and longing for nothing so much as a bath and bed. When she arrived home at last she was relieved to see that Zelda had already turned in, exhausted, probably, after the long day. Hannah felt a twinge of guilt over not having done more to help. Guilt was becoming a familiar feeling, she thought ruefully. She glanced at Sam who slept in the kitchen now, then hurried up to her own room, where she went straight to her work table, spreading out notes and pictures and settling down at her word processor. Then she hesitated, closing her eyes briefly and trying to will herself into a mood of concentration. Trying to shut out all thoughts of sun-browned hands, tender smiles, laughter, passion and kisses that seemed to shut out the whole world. *Back to business, Hannah,* a small firm voice told her. Opening her eyes, she took a deep breath and began to work.

At one o'clock she stood up and stretched, switched off her desk lamp and walked to the open window where a soft night breeze was blowing the curtain inward. For a long time she remained there, looking at the lawn silvered by moonlight, at the dark masses of trees. One part of her was tired, but another part recognized that sleep would be slow in coming if she went to bed now. She thought for a moment, then tiptoed to her door and opened it, stealing out into the hall and down the steps. She let herself out the front door quietly, and with slow footsteps traced her way along the moonlit path that led toward Jake's house. Memories seemed to walk with her, crowding into her mind, flooding and spilling over into a hodgepodge of everything that had happened since the day she'd arrived in Harrison Falls.

This was where she'd walked that first afternoon, dressed in her city clothes and feeling strange, an outsider. And how many times since then had she walked this path? That first night when they'd all trooped over to help deliver the puppies. Carrie's birthday party, with Jake's eyes meeting hers across the table. The wild rainstorm she'd run through to take care of Foxfire. The memory of that day and how it had ended in passionate embraces with the sweet-smelling hay all around them brought a lump to her throat.

She reached the hedge and pushed her way through. Ahead of her his house was dark and silent, but in the yard she could see the outlines of Carrie's hives and hear, distantly, the faint murmur of fanning wings. *They're keeping the queen cool and comfortable,* Carrie had explained to her once. Hannah stood quietly in the darkness, letting feelings and emotions wash over her.

There was movement from the shadows at the corner of the yard, someone stepping forward. Hannah gave a start of fright.

"I remember how you walked over here the day you arrived," Jake said. His voice was quiet and reminiscent but Hannah could hear a sharp bitter edge, too, that cut like a knife through the still night air. He was standing with his hands in the pockets of his jeans. The moonlight caught in his tousled hair and threw his face into planes and shadows that looked unfamiliar, not like his daytime features.

"I . . . I didn't feel like sleeping just now," Hannah stammered. "I had to come out for some air."

"I can understand why you might have trouble sleeping," he said dryly. Then he resumed his low, thoughtful tone. "It was right about there, wasn't it, where you fell when Zack came at you—and then you got stung and I had to take you inside and get the stinger out."

Pain twisted inside Hannah. "I imagine it was all the excitement of the picnic today," she went on, trying to stick to her excuse. "I wasn't the least bit sleepy. . . ."

He turned toward her and she could feel him looming over her, his eyes strange, hooded. "I suppose it's right that we say goodbye here—the same place we met," he said, and the bitterness seemed to intensify. "This is goodbye, isn't it?" Hannah remained wretchedly silent, unable to speak. He shook his head. "I sure had you figured wrong, Hannah."

Hannah's breath came out in a small sigh. "Yes, I guess you did," she whispered. She was feeling curiously numb as she listened in the country quiet to the shrilling of insects and the soft whisper of the tree branches overhead.

"But you were right all along," he said in a cold, tight voice. "You said you didn't want people to get too close to you. You said it wouldn't work. You were right on the mark."

"I don't belong here," Hannah murmured.

"Right again," he said crisply.

Had she done the thing so badly? Hannah felt a stab of pain mixed with remorse. Could she have managed better? But now it was too late. She was in the very vortex of the thing, the outcome still far from certain. She had to see it through. And if it all blew up in her face, at least she would be the one in the middle, not Jake. From the beginning she had only wanted to protect him, to hold the town together. Had she been wrong?

"Jake, I'm sorry about the way things turned out," she said, and for a moment, as they stood there close together in the dark she thought he might reach out to her, tilt her head back and cover her mouth in a kiss that would consume them both, that would put everything right between them. Instead he gave her a long hard look with those shadowed eyes and then abruptly turned away.

"Goodbye, Hannah," he said brusquely, striding into the darkness.

It was late Sunday morning before Hannah made her way down to the kitchen. She had not slept until dawn, and then only fitfully. The glimpse she'd had of her own face in the mirror when she arose was of a pale stranger with dark smudges around the eyes. Yet she was feeling curiously numb, and with the numbness had come a kind of calm. She had only to get through today, she reminded herself. Only today, and then she could leave Harrison Falls and all its memories behind her. She poured herself a cup of coffee and sank down at the table. Moments later she heard the pickup roaring into the driveway, and Zelda came in, wearing her Sunday hat and one of her flowered print dresses, which all managed, somehow, to look alike.

"Well, there you are," Zelda said cheerfully, but Hannah knew she had seen the paleness, the dark circles. "I just let you sleep when I left for church. Thought you probably needed it."

"Wonderful picnic yesterday," Hannah said, struggling to sound normal, but even her voice was strange to her—distant and unfamiliar.

"Oh, yes, everyone had a good time, I think. Now, before I forget, you had a call this morning. A Mr. Anderson in New York City."

"Bob? He called here?"

"Yes, but I was determined not to wake you, so I took the message. He said could you drive back tonight in time to testify tomorrow. Said to be sure you got the message and I said he wasn't to worry. You might want to call him back, though."

Hannah nodded slowly.

"I sure do hope this isn't the last time we see you," Zelda said, her voice faltering slightly. "I mean, it's meant so much to all of us, having you here this summer. It was just...real nice." She eyed Hannah obliquely, then looked away again. "Well, my stars, I've got to change and think about getting back there to the church. Ed Jackson brought the chairs back in his truck after the picnic and nobody thought to clean 'em off. Most have ice cream stuck to 'em, and mustard. I've got some of the Sunday-school kids coming to help—"

"I love him, Zelda," Hannah interrupted suddenly.

Zelda unpinned her hat and took it off, sinking down on a chair across the table from Hannah. "Shoot, anybody can see that," she said gently. "But then why...?"

Hannah was shaking her head slowly. "I've always made a mess of relationships."

Zelda considered this. "Well, yes, I guess showing up at the picnic with Walker Harrison didn't do that particular relationship any good. I don't know just why it happened, but couldn't you and Jake work things out somehow?"

Hannah looked away, out through the window where the big pine tree rustled its branches against the screen. "I don't belong here, Zelda," she said almost in a whisper.

"Oh, now that's nonsense," Zelda said flatly. "I never saw anybody belong more." She was silent for a moment as a noisy fly buzzed against the screen. "But you do what you have to do," she said, her voice soft. "I know there're things going on here I don't know anything about."

Hannah looked back at her, and tears threatened to spill over her lower lids. "Thanks, Zelda," she said in a throaty whisper. "Thanks for everything." Then she stood up. "I'd better start packing."

After she'd put her things together hurriedly she made two telephone calls, one to Bob Anderson in New York, reassuring him that she'd be back in plenty of time to appear in court, and another one to Walker Harrison.

"I'm driving to New York tonight," she told him, making her voice as bright as possible. "Something came up, so I didn't have much notice. Could we have coffee together before I leave?"

"You bet! Hey, I hate to see you leave, Hannah. What time shall I pick you up?"

"I still have a few things to do. How about if we just meet somewhere? Millie's Luncheonette out on Route 7—how would that be?"

"You're sounding more and more like a native. That'd be fine."

"I'll be there in about a half hour."

Hannah went back upstairs to her room, her eyes skimming over the packed luggage. Then she sat down at her worktable for the last time, writing a note, addressing an envelope and sticking a stamp on it. She gathered the pile of photos and a small disk from her computer, which she put in her shoulder bag. Finally she slipped out of the room, stopping in the kitchen only long enough to see that Sam was properly fed, watered and penned in his little corner. She leaned over and stroked the smooth head gently before straightening up and leaving the house. Zelda had already gone back to the church on her cleanup errand. "But don't you dare leave until I get back," she'd warned on her way out the door.

Hannah kept her eyes resolutely away from the McCabe house as she got into the white Porsche and headed out onto the county highway. She drove into the village and stopped at the post office, slipping the envelope she'd addressed into the outside mailbox, then proceeding through town and out toward Route 7.

Walker Harrison was there ahead of her, already sitting in a booth in the small roadside luncheonette. There were red-and-white checked plastic mats on the table. On the counter stood large, transparent plate covers revealing doughnuts and pies. Millie, the stout proprietor, was bustling about behind the counter, and several of the tables were occupied. Hannah slid into the booth across the table from Walker.

"I'm sorry to hear you're returning to New York," Walker said. "I hope that's not going to be forever." He looked fresh and casual in a navy knit shirt and white cotton trousers, and his smile when he saw her was alight with genuine pleasure. "Seeing you twice in one weekend, though, is a real treat."

A waitress in a checked apron that matched the place mats came and took their order for coffee. When she'd left, Hannah said quietly, "I'm afraid you won't think it such a treat when you hear what I have to say, Walker."

His eyebrows drew together in a puzzled look, but his smile remained fixed. "Oh, come on. What could be so bad?"

Hannah took a deep breath as she opened her bag and removed the envelope of pictures and the small computer disk. She fanned out the pictures on the table and waited for his reaction. "That's one roll," she said. "The second roll is still in my camera, but it contains some very nice shots of you passing money to the man from Acme Disposal. I managed to get his truck in the pictures, too."

Walker's smile had faded and his face had gone pale. For several moments he said nothing. He stared in stunned silence at the photographs. The waitress returned with two cups of coffee and placed them on the table, glancing curiously at their faces before she left. At last Walker seemed to collect himself. "How did you... What made you do all this?" he demanded in a harsh, low voice. "What business is it of yours?"

"Ah. That's just the point," Hannah said easily. "A story is always my business, and I knew this was a story from the first moment I saw that place. It was the day the hunt club went out on the working party."

He stared at her incredulously, shaking his head and letting out a low groan. "Just my luck—I had to meet a crusading newspaperwoman. Of all the rotten breaks." He leaned forward, elbows on the table, his head in his hands. "I suppose there's more to this. What are you planning to do about it?"

"I've already done it." Hannah's voice was firm and controlled. "I've written the story." She held out the disk. "It's all on here, and a duplicate disk has just been mailed to my editor in New York, with instructions that he's not to run it until I give him the go-ahead."

"But you know nothing about the situation! You're just jumping to conclusions!" Walker protested, dropping his hands and looking at her, his face dark with anger. "There's absolutely nothing wrong with the way that waste is being disposed of!"

"Then you haven't a thing to worry about, have you?" Hannah smiled pleasantly at him and sipped her coffee. "And when the man arrives from the state environmental office you can just explain it to him."

"What man?" Walker's scowl blackened.

"The one I called the other day. He agreed that the matter should be looked into."

For a moment Walker was silent, still glowering at her. Then his mouth drew into a sarcastic line. "That's why you were so anxious to go to the picnic with me, wasn't it? So you could come to the factory and snoop around?"

Hannah's shoulders lifted in a small shrug. "A reporter has to use the means at hand," she said lightly. "I didn't expect it to pay off so handsomely, but I'm glad it did. It made the story easier to put together."

"What do you expect me to do?" he asked through clenched teeth. "I suppose you've made that your business, too."

"That's easy. I expect you to make it right. And I'm sure there'll be no repercussions if you explain that to Mr. Haverhill, the man from the state environmental office. Here's his number, by the way. You may want to call him. The sooner he comes and sees it, the sooner you can start putting things right. He'll tell you what steps to take. Oh, and of course there's the matter of restitution. If I were you I'd do it all quickly and quietly, before anybody catches on and starts thinking about lawsuits."

"What do you mean?" Walker stared at her.

"Well, some people have been hurt by your actions. The Rittenmyers, for one. They've lost three calves already, and I don't think it would be hard to prove that it's the result of the cows drinking contaminated water that flows directly from your property. That represents a substantial loss for the Rittenmyers, which I'm sure you'll want to put right."

The look he was shooting her was pure hatred, cold and razor sharp. Hannah found herself strangely impervious to it. She returned his gaze coolly, surveying him with critical detachment, noting the casual designer clothing, the blown-dry hair, the expression of self-indulgence, comparing it in her mind with the kindly Peyton Harrison in his white suit at the Founder's Day picnic as he opened the ceremonies. The old gentleman was proud of his family's contributions to the town, proud of his place as its first citizen. Well loved, respected by everyone. How had he managed to produce a son with no scruples whatsoever?

"You're lucky," she said quietly. "You're lucky I was the one to get hold of this. I respect your father and I know how much he's done for this town. I've come to love Harrison Falls, and I don't want to see it pulled apart by a scandal like this. And you're lucky, too, that I stopped you before it got really serious. Three calves is bad enough—next time it might be children. If toxic substances started seeping into the town's water supply, so Mr. Haverhill said—"

"All right, all right. Spare me the moralizing."

She looked at him curiously. "I just wonder why you did it," she said idly. "Perhaps because you weren't the manager your father was, right? And maybe the business wasn't showing the profits it used to? You started cutting corners in every direction, I'll bet. That included getting rid of your dangerous waste products the cheapest way you could—by creating your own dump site." She picked up the pictures and disk from the table, returning them to her handbag.

As she rose to leave, he asked suddenly, "Wait a minute. Does everyone in town know about this?"

"No," she said coldly. "No one knows."

"Not even Jake McCabe?" His mouth twisted in a sneer as he said it.

Hannah took a deep breath, trying to ignore the shaft of pain that shot through her at the sound of his name.

"No one," she repeated as she turned and left.

CHAPTER ELEVEN

ZELDA, BACK IN her familiar jeans and outsize man's shirt, watched Hannah move around the bedroom, opening drawers and checking under the bed.

"I have the darnedest way of leaving slippers behind," Hannah remarked.

"I'll be sure to send on anything I find," Zelda said. Her plain face had lost its usual smile. Her mouth was tucked in at the corners as if she was holding back emotion.

"I know I don't need to say anything about Sam," Hannah went on brightly. "He'll probably drive you crazy, but I know how much he loves you...." She stopped as her voice turned wavery.

"He'll miss you like blazes," Zelda said. "But I'll take him to my room at night with me."

"I'm sure you'll spoil him thoroughly." Hannah smiled. She moved to the window where she had so often stood. "I love the view from here," she said softly. "The backyard and that border of flowers, whatever they are..."

"Hollyhocks," Zelda supplied.

"And then the trees way out there at the edge..."

"I hope you'll come back sometime," Zelda said. "I hate to think we'd never see you again."

"Oh, goodness, who knows? But we'll keep in touch—of course we will." Even as she said it, Hannah hated the words. They sounded like the end of a business lunch, brittle and meaningless. "Leslie Harte said if I ever came back I'd see a lot of changes. She talked about the house and clinic Jake's going to have outside of town." She glanced around at Zelda.

"My stars, things don't change that fast in Harrison Falls," Zelda said, reaching in her pocket for a large handkerchief and blowing her nose loudly. "Anyway, maybe that's all the more reason for you to come back—to keep track of what's happening here."

Hannah smiled, a small rueful smile. "I think there may be people here who won't be so anxious to see me back, Zelda."

The older woman studied her sharply. "Well, there's plenty of us who *will* want to see you."

"Oh, and will you tell Carrie I said goodbye?" Hannah asked. "Tell her I didn't forget about her dress. I'm going to send her one from New York."

Zelda nodded. "I'll tell her."

For a moment the two women looked at one another across the room. Then Hannah crossed to her and Zelda opened her arms and held her tight.

"Goodbye, Zelda," Hannah whispered, and pulled away.

THE APARTMENT overlooking Central Park had always seemed bright and airy. Now, returning to it after Zelda's big old house with its high ceilings, clean laundry piled on chairs, ringing telephone, baking smells and general air of haphazard comfort, Hannah thought the apartment looked strangely constricted, boxed in. But she'd get used to it again in no time, she told herself. And in fact she had very little chance to reflect on this or any other concern, for almost at once she was thrown into a whirlwind of activity, with Bob Anderson, stocky and determined, shepherding her through and running interference.

She even became accustomed to the sight of her own face on the six o'clock news each night. "Crusading reporter Hannah Chase left the courthouse today after a grueling day of testimony against contractors and building inspectors accused of fraud and conspiracy in a multimillion dollar scam..." "Miss Chase spoke briefly with reporters, referring other questions to her newspaper's attorney..." "Hannah Chase, whose articles last winter lifted the lid on corruption in the building industry..."

"Relax, it'll all die down in a little while," Bob Anderson reassured her, tilting back in his chair and putting both feet on his desk.

"A goldfish has more privacy," Hannah fumed.

"You're just about out of it. They've got your testimony and that's all they needed. Pretty soon nobody'll even recognize you on the street."

"And the cop outside my apartment door? Do I really need all that protection?"

"That, too, shall pass." He grinned. "Look here, what about this story you sent me from Harrison Mills?"

"Harrison *Falls*," she corrected him. "What about it?"

"Sounds good. Why can't we run it? Not front page, maybe, but in our news-around-the-state section."

"Because the problem's been solved. I called the man in the environmental office and the cleanup's already under way."

He wagged a finger at her. "You're letting somebody off the hook, sweetie. It's not like you."

"Trust me on this one, Bob," she said. "There are times when it's better to solve a problem quietly."

He studied her. "Liked that little burg, didn't you?"

"It was a nice place," she said haltingly. "For a vacation."

"Well, the stories you sent from there were some of the best work you've ever done." He was still scrutinizing her. After a moment he said thoughtfully, "You know, Hannah, people can make a difference anyplace. New York isn't the whole world. Take this story you sent about the toxic waste. All right, you won't let me use it, but it made a difference, didn't it? Lives were changed because of it."

She breathed out slowly. "Yes, lives were changed all right."

He seemed about to say more, then changed tack. "What do you think about Alaska?"

Her eyes widened. "Alaska!"

"Well, sure. Why not? How'd you like to go up there—still some summer left. You could do an in-depth piece for us. See Anchorage, Fairbanks, Valdez—I hear that's a real boomtown since the big spill—watch the salmon run off Bristol Bay, visit some of those old Russian village churches. Only a hundred and some miles from Siberia in spots."

"Oh, I don't know, Bob...."

"Well, why don't you give it some thought?"

She got to her feet wearily, lifting her hair from her nape. "I will, I promise. Right now I have an errand to do, and then I'm heading for home and a hot bath."

The shop where the taxi let her off was on Fifth Avenue. Hannah glanced at the window display hurriedly, then ducked inside, ignoring the occasional puzzled or curious glances that followed her as people tried to remember where they'd seen her face. She was becoming used to it.

"I'd like to see something suitable for a thirteen-year-old," she said to the saleswoman who approached her.

It took only a few minutes to select a dress for Carrie. Turquoise—she remembered how Carrie had admired the turquoise jumpsuit she'd worn that first night—and with a simple dropped waist and a flat bow at one side.

"Here's the address where I want it sent," she said, writing it out. "Please see that it's delivered as quickly as possible."

By the end of two weeks the case had gone to the jury, with almost no one in doubt about the outcome. Hannah was relieved to have dropped out of the news, and felt only a small regret at losing the officer who had stayed outside her door so faithfully. At least he'd been someone to say hello to. Bob Anderson had supplied her with pamphlets and books on Alaska, which she pored over dutifully. Another time, she thought, it would have appealed to her, but now she felt a curious indifference.

Then one evening she began looking through her bookshelves for something to read, skimming over titles and authors, seeking some old favorite, when the doorbell rang.

She glanced up, hesitating briefly. Not that she was really worried, but now that Officer Blake was no longer assigned to her... She squared her shoulders and approached the door, making sure the chain was secure before opening the door a crack.

"Yes?" she said, and saw Jake standing there. For a moment she could only stare through the small gap. Then with fumbling fingers she released the chain.

"Jake!" She opened the door wide and stood looking at him, all her emotions suddenly turned upside down. Blood sang in her veins and warmth seemed to reach from her toes to the very roots of her hair.

"May I come in?" His face was stern and unsmiling.

"Yes, of course—I mean, please do come in. What in the world . . . ?"

He stepped inside. His eyes didn't leave her face. They seemed to be studying her, reaching into her very depths. "How could you do it, Hannah?" he asked.

"Do—" Hannah found herself without speech. Had the worst happened then? Had the whole matter come out in the open, after all, and had the town pulled itself apart with bitterness and name-calling? She had tried so hard!

"How could you leave without telling me the truth?" he said in a low voice.

"What's happened?" she managed to whisper.

His mouth moved slightly, forming a sardonic smile. "Harrison Falls is to have a new municipal park and picnic ground. Donated by the Harrison family—outside of town on a plot of ground, which was being used as a dump."

"Oh. I see." Hannah breathed out softly.

"Walker Harrison, public-spirited fellow that he is, feels it would serve a better purpose that way. A man from the state environmental office has been conferring with him on the project. I suspect this guy—a Mr. Haverhill—will be policing it like a bulldog, doing tests to make sure it's safe and keeping one eye on Walker, too."

Hannah's sigh of relief was audible now. "That's good. I'm so glad."

"Also, Harv Rittenmyer's recently bought three new cows and a prize bull. Several thousand dollars' investment there."

"Really."

He studied her face, blue eyes fixed on it as if to memorize every feature. "Hannah, I've figured out that the waste being dumped was dangerous. Obviously you did, too, but well before me—you could have told me."

She bit her lower lip. "Does anyone else in town know?"

"Zelda, of course. It didn't take much for the two of us to figure it out. We've both known Walker Harrison for a long time. He's not given to spontaneous generosity. It was your doing, wasn't it, Hannah? How did you manage it?"

"I took pictures. I wrote a story. I confronted him with what I'd learned and what I suspected."

"And the day of the picnic?"

She smiled bitterly. "That was when I got my best pictures."

"If I'd only known—"

"Suppose I'd been wrong? I knew you didn't like Walker. It would have put you squarely in the middle of an awful town squabble."

He shook his head hopelessly, still not taking his eyes from her face. "Carrie loved the dress," he said softly.

"How is she?"

"Great. In California right now. I never did know how you talked her into that."

"I didn't have to talk her into it. She wanted to go. She just needed someone to help her see it."

He leaned over and for the first time she noticed he was carrying a small bag in one hand. He placed it on the floor and out of its open top a small furry head appeared.

"Sam!" Hannah knelt down and picked up the puppy. "Oh, you've grown! I hardly know you!"

She stood up with Sam licking her face enthusiastically and was at once enveloped in a pair of strong arms. "Can we dispense with Sam for a minute?" he murmured, setting the puppy on the floor. Then he pulled her close and brought his mouth against hers in a long demanding kiss that Hannah realized she'd been thirsting for ever since she'd left Harrison Falls. She returned his passion with an intensity that had been building all that time.

"It was partly my fault," he murmured presently, close to her ear. "I held back, too. I never really told you how much I loved you. Even that day in the barn, the day it rained, I don't think you really believed I meant it with all my heart—that it was for always as far as I was concerned."

"Oh, Jake—" Her mouth found his again, and it was a long moment before he said softly, "It sure would be a shame if Carrie only got to wear that dress to one wedding."

"Oh, Jake, are you sure?" Hannah pulled back, searching his face anxiously.

"You mean because you're a city girl? Honestly, I'm willing to overlook that," he said with a twinkle.

HARLEQUIN
Romance®

Coming Next Month

#3109 EVERY WOMAN'S DREAM Bethany Campbell
Cal Buchanan's photograph landed on Tess's desk like manna from heaven. It would guarantee the success of the calendar project that could launch Tess in New York's advertising world. Only things don't work out quite that way—there are complications....

#3110 FAIR TRIAL Elizabeth Duke
They come from two different worlds, Tanya Barrington and Simon Devlin, two lawyers who have to work together on a case. Their clashes are inevitable—and their attraction to each other is undeniable.

#3111 THE GIRL HE LEFT BEHIND Emma Goldrick
Molly and Tim were childhood friends, and he never knew that he'd broken Molly's heart when he married her cousin. When Tim turns up on Molly's doorstep with his daughter, asking for help, Molly takes them in despite the pain they bring her. And the joy . . .

#3112 AN IMPOSSIBLE PASSION Stephanie Howard
Fayiz Davidian's job offer comes just when Giselle needs it, and if he thinks she'll refuse just because she finds him arrogant and overbearing, he's dead wrong. She always rises to a challenge!

#3113 FIRST COMES MARRIAGE Debbie Macomber
Janine Hartman's grandfather and Zach Thomas have merged their companies. Now Gramps wants to arrange another kind of merger—a wedding between his unwilling granddaughter and an equally unwilling Zach!

#3114 HIDDEN HEART Jessica Steele
To protect her sister and family, Mornay shoulders the blame when wealthy industrialist Brad Kendrick wrongly accuses her of being the hit-and-run driver who'd landed him in the hospital. She never suspects that her heart will become involved....

Available in March wherever paperback books are sold, or through Harlequin Reader Service:

In the U.S.
P.O. Box 1397
Buffalo, N.Y.
14240-1397

In Canada
P.O. Box 603
Fort Erie, Ontario
L2A 5X3

COMING IN 1991 FROM HARLEQUIN SUPERROMANCE:

Three abandoned orphans,
one missing heiress!

Dying millionaire Owen Byrnside receives an anonymous letter informing him that twenty-six years ago, his son, Christopher, fathered a daughter. The infant was abandoned at a foundling home that subsequently burned to the ground, destroying all records. Three young women could be Owen's long-lost granddaughter, and Owen is determined to track down each of them! Read their stories in

#434 HIGH STAKES (available January 1991)
#438 DARK WATERS (available February 1991)
#442 BRIGHT SECRETS (available March 1991)

Three exciting stories of intrigue and romance by veteran Superromance author Jane Silverwood.

They went in through the terrace door. The house was dark, most of the servants were down at the circus, and only Nelbert's hired security guards were in sight. It was child's play for Blackheart to move past them, the work of two seconds to go through the solid lock on the terrace door. And then they were creeping through the darkened house, up the long curving stairs, Ferris fully as noiseless as the more experienced Blackheart.

They stopped on the second floor landing. "What if they have guns?" Ferris mouthed silently.

Blackheart shrugged. "Then duck."

"How reassuring," she responded. Footsteps directly above them signaled that the thieves were on the move, and so should they be.

For more romance, suspense and adventure, read Harlequin Intrigue. Two exciting titles each month, available wherever Harlequin Books are sold.